PATRICIA THAYER

THE COLTON CREEK COWBOY

To my readers,

This is the third book in the Slater Sister's series, ***Colton Creek Cowboy,*** but there will be a few differences this time.

First, I've moved from Montana, to the old Colton Creek Homestead in Wyoming. There Tori Slater plans to move on with her life, and away from her stalking ex-boyfriend. She gets help from ranch's caretaker, Logan McNeely.

Second, I'm now INDIE published. That doesn't mean that my style or my stories will change. I'll continue to write the small town, family stories, and as of now, I'm concentrating on finishing this series with Tori's and Marissa's stories. And maybe I'll even add in the two brothers, Quintin and Rafael.

I've also completed Colt and Lucia's story which I hope to have out by the first of next year. Their love story began 30 years earlier when they met at a rodeo. Not just any rodeo, but the Daddy of 'em all, Frontier Days in Cheyenne Wyoming in 1983. Colt was walking along the midway before his saddle bronc event when he looked up and first saw Lucia Delgado trapped on the Ferris wheel. He didn't exactly rescue her, but he was waiting for her by the time she reached the ground. ***Love Struck Cowboy*** will be out early in 2014.

Thank you, readers, for your loyalty over the years. And I hope you continue this new journey with me along with some new reader. You can keep up on any news by going to my website *www.patriciathayer.com* or on facebook to Patricia Thayer Wright.

Colton Creek Cowboy

Copyright 2013 Patricia Wright
Published by Patricia Thayer
Cover design by Ann Proyous
Formatted by Author's HQ

For more information on the author and her works, please see www.PatriciaThayer.com

DEDICATION

To my friends who convinced me to take this leap, and for helping me realize, you're never too old for a new adventure. And to Steve, you're the only one I want to share this adventure with.

CHAPTER ONE

Some people would say she was running away; she liked to think of herself as heading toward a new life.

Vittoria Slater drove under the archway that read, Colton Creek Ranch. She continued along the narrow road past a barn, several white outbuildings, and a large horse corral. The place all looked well kept. Then she turned her attention up the hill and to the house.

"Let's hope it's in the same condition," she murmured. Tori steered her small SUV up the gravel driveway and parked in front of the huge, two-story log cabin. The old Colton family homestead. The imposing one-hundred-and-ten-year-old structure was weathered and faded from the brutal Wyoming weather, and the large porch tilted precariously. She doubted any work had been done on the place since the last century. That was the last time a family member had lived in the place her great-great-grandparents, Cyrus and Rachel Colton homesteaded.

Now the place, a place she hadn't even heard about until a few days ago, would be her new home. According to her father, Colt Slater, this northern section of the state was prime grazing land when Rachel and Cy homesteaded here.

One of the questions Tori needed to get an answer for her family was, would running a larger cattle herd here be profitable enough to keep paying for the state land lease? Or did they proceed like at the ranch in Montana, where they'd found other alternatives for income, like opening up the area to anglers and hunters?

That was only one of the reasons Tori was here. Besides the answers to her questions, Tori needed to see the caretaker, some old guy by the name of Nate McNeely. However, the true reason she volunteered for the trip was to get away from her overprotective family. Her sisters, Ana and Josie, were on the top of that list. Time for her to strike out on her own, and gain some independence. What better place than an isolated ranch in northern Wyoming? No one would find her here.

Tori climbed out of her car and stretched out the kinks as she glanced at the beautiful backdrop of the Big Horn Mountains, then toward the miles of open range in every direction. These pastures were painted a rich green from the early spring rains. On the drive, she remembered passing streams overflowing from the mountain snow pack.

After years of living in Southern California, she would be happy with no traffic and a little solitude. The fewer people, the better. She wanted a quiet place to stay for awhile and regroup.

Tori started toward the house. Even though her family had called ahead to let the caretaker know of her arrival, she told herself not to expect too much. All she hoped for was a bed to sleep in, some internet access so she could work, maybe a horse so she could look around the place. These little necessities would make her a happy camper.

Leaving Los Angeles, and going back home to her childhood Montana home, the Lazy S Ranch, hadn't been her idea. Nor was the spot her first choice to hide out. That was the reason she'd volunteered to come to Wyoming. She needed a place where no one knew her, or how to find her. A place to live until she again felt safe, so she could think and decide where to go next.

What better place than where her ancestors first settled in northern Wyoming? The Colton side of the family anyway; the Slaters had settled in southern Montana. The next generation of families merged with the marriage of George Slater and Millie Colton.

Tori was excited as she walked up the steps and carefully made her way across the sheet of plywood that covered what look like a rotted wood floor. She made a mental note to talk to the caretaker as to why it wasn't ever fixed. She tried the iron handle and the heavy oak door swung open with a squeak. As her gaze swept the area, she stepped across the threshold.

Inside was dim, but she could see it was one massive room with a kitchen off to one corner, and a huge stone fireplace on the other side. Upon further investigation, she found a small bathroom and bedroom downstairs. A wrought-iron banister led to a second floor where an open railing circling half the downstairs. She looked up at the high-pitched ceiling supported by exposed beams. Pulling back the heavy drapes from the windows made dust fly everywhere. Tori brushed the dirt from her hands onto her jeans.

"So I'll be cleaning for a few days."

Excitement fueled her and she began to strip the protective sheets off a faded floral sofa and two brown leather chairs.

Her artist's eye took over and moving through the room, she could begin to see the potential of this place. She checked the light switch and was grateful the lamp over the table went on. No television, but she could live without one.

She started upstairs and her tennis shoes were silent, except for the squeaks on the third and fifth steps. The wide hallway made finding the first bedroom easy. Not a bad size. Her footsteps echoed across the bare floor as she walked to the row of windows and a built-in wooden bench. She sat and looked out over the ranch. A small herd of cattle grazed in the pasture. "Not a bad view." Peaceful. Something she hadn't had much of in a long time.

She scanned the view and didn't see another home or building, just open prairie. The question was, could she live out here by herself? She was determined. Right now, this option was better than dealing with the issues she'd left behind. Memories of a father who never wanted his daughters loomed heavily in her decision to come here. Although Colt had sworn he wanted to make up for those bad years, Tori still wasn't sure she could manage a father-daughter relationship after twenty five years.

Even though he was nearly fully recovered now, his recent stroke made her realize how temporary life was. Then on top of the other garbage in her life, her mother showed up after a twenty-five year absence. All Tori wanted was to get away, so she could figure out a way to move on with her life, both personal and professional.

A thump sounded and Tori froze as fear took over. *Stop it! No one knows you're here besides the family.* Another thud resonated from the other bedroom. Her heart drummed in her ears, but she walked out and bravely started down the hall, reassuring herself that all kinds of noises sounded in an old house. Her maniac ex-boyfriend couldn't possibly be here.

The floor creaked as she walked to the closed door. With a shaky hand, she reached for the brass doorknob and slowly pushed it open. Suddenly, someone jerked from the other side.

"What?" She went flying into the room, but quickly stopped when she ran into a large, solid body. She gasped and looked up into light green eyes that stared back, sending a jolt through her. A dark shadow covered his jaw, making him look menacing.

Heart pounding double time, she stepped back and examined the unfamiliar man dressed in a denim jacket over a tan, collared shirt that covered broad shoulders and chest. A pair of dark jeans encased his long legs. On his feet were cowboy boots, adding an inch to his already intimidating height. And he was too young to be the caretaker.

She took another step back. Trying to regain composure, she questioned, "Who are you? What are you doing here?"

Logan McNeely was caught off guard by this woman's dark beauty. A pretty heart-shaped face was surrounded by long, shiny black hair. He stopped the direction of his thoughts. She was a nice enough package to turn a man's head. Any man but him.

He already knew who this was. But he didn't like his sudden reaction to her. "You must be Tori Slater."

She nodded. "Yes, I'm Colt's daughter. Are you Nate McNeely?"

"I'm a McNeely, but I'm Logan. Nate was my grandfather. He passed away last fall."

"Oh, I'm sorry." That seemed to frazzle her as she looked toward the bed. "I don't believe my father knew that, but he's been recovering from a stroke."

He thought about three years ago. It was the last time he'd seen Colt Slater. "I heard about your father's stroke. How is he doing?"

She smiled. "He's coming along." She looked around at the half made four-poster bed and her eyebrows rose. "So, are you living in this house?"

"No. When here, I stay in the apartment over the bunkhouse."

"Oh, okay." She looked relieved.

"To tell the truth, I was expecting Vance Rivers. He was supposed to come and stay."

"Sorry, last minute change of plans."

No kidding. He'd gotten the surprise call yesterday from Rivers the foreman at the Lazy S, telling him his sister-in-law, Tori Slater, was coming to the ranch.

Damn. He'd been here three years, his grandfather over twenty years, and no one gave a fig about what went on at Colton Creek. He had hoped the situation would stay that way, but now, she showed up.

"So, Mr. McNeely," She began as she folded her arms over his chest. "I didn't expect to find anyone here in the house."

"I wasn't expecting anyone until tomorrow. I'm just dropping off a load of clean sheets and towels." He shrugged. "Clara Williams brought them by when she heard you were coming. She was going to help clean up some, but there wasn't time."

"That was nice of her. Does she work here, too?"

"No, she owns the general store in town where I got the message about your arrival."

"Message? You mean there isn't any phone service?"

"There is, but the landline hasn't been hooked up for years. If you have a cell phone that should be okay and there's internet. I have a wireless connection, and you're welcome to use it during your stay. Do you know how long that will be?"

"I'm not sure, a week or two, maybe more. Is there a problem with me staying here?"

He shook his head. "Your family owns the place. Why would I object?"

"We might own the place, but your grandfather has been running it for a lot of years."

And the Slaters owned it. Somehow Nate and Colt had managed to have a good friendship over the years. But things have changed because Logan wanted more.

He nodded toward the big bed. "Since you're here, I'll let you finish making up the bed yourself." He looked down at his large hands. "You'd probably do a better job."

"Thank you for starting it," she said and stepped next to the aged cedar frame.

He headed for the door and stopped. "Eggs, bacon and milk are in the refrigerator. I didn't have a chance to do much else."

"I didn't even expect you to do this much, Mr. McNeely, but thank you."

"Not a problem." He walked out.

She noticed he wore spurs and leather chaps. Mr. Cowboy must have been out with the herd.

Once she heard the door close, she felt relief and quickly finished up the bed, went down to the kitchen, and turned on more lights. She stared at the old, chipped appliances and stained cupboards. This place needed a good cleaning. Moving in a circle on the worn linoleum floor, she noticed there wasn't a microwave, either. And takeout was out of the question.

Looked like she would truly be roughing it in Wyoming. She thought about the cowboy who came along with this ranch. Okay, he'd frightened her at first and was a little gruff. He was probably just not used to having people around, and all she cared about was if he did his job.

Hopefully, she could do hers. Problem was she wasn't quite sure if coming here would solve anything.

***

Two hours later, Tori had finished unloading her car and put away her clothes, then she ate a late lunch. Not knowing how long she'd be here, she called and signed up for basic satellite internet service. Maybe buying a small flat screen television wouldn't be a bad idea. She only hoped there was a store in the small town of Dawson Springs.

If her family was going to change this place into another guest lodge, like the River's Edge

Lodge in Montana, she needed to find out what they could offer in amenities. How was the fishing? Was there a place for swimming, hiking trails, and horseback riding?

She sat down at the scarred kitchen table, and picked up her phone and called home. After it rang three times, she got the recording, remembering it was Kathleen, the housekeeper's day off.

"Yea, everyone, it's me, Tori. I made it to Colton Creek Ranch without any problems. I'm settling in the cabin and planning to have a look around tomorrow. Talk to you soon. Bye.

She punched the button and ended the call. Since her twin sister, Josie, was off on her honeymoon with her new husband, Garrett, she didn't expect to hear from her any time soon. That was a good thing. Tori wanted to be on her own, and since her break up with Dane and all the trouble he'd caused, her family had been hovering over her. The chance to come to Wyoming had been a godsend. So she didn't want to let her family down.

Tori put on her denim jacket and headed outside to feel a cool breeze brush back her hair. She wanted to look over the place before she lost daylight. If the family planned to keep this ranch going, they needed to see a profit. And just running cattle wasn't doing it. She might have been living in Los Angeles for the past seven years, but she was still the daughter of a rancher. She'd learned a few things growing up on the Lazy S.

Her thoughts turned to Logan McNeely. She wondered if her father knew much about him. Had he stepped into his grandfather's job without discussing the matter with Colt? Nate had been gone about six months; his death happening about the same time that Colt had his stroke. So if her father knew, the fact was something he never told anyone, or it could have been a memory that never came back.

And what exactly was Logan's job here? She had a lot of questions.

She walked across the yard to the large, glossy white barn. So some things had been well kept. Inside the warmth was soothing as were the familiar smells: a mixture of horses, manure and fresh straw. She'd missed all this. Especially, she missed the quiet and the solitude. The fast pace never stopped in LA. Everyone just kept going, day and night. Being here would be a nice change.

She glanced around to see that the inside was as well kept as the outside. The stalls were nearly new and the bales of straw were neatly stacked off in a dry area.

After finding a handful of carrots in a bin, she set off to introduce herself to the residents. In the first stall stood a big chestnut stallion about sixteen hands high. A white blaze crossed his face.

"Oh, aren't you a beauty. Hey, big guy." She rubbed the animal's soft muzzle when he stuck his head over the gate. He blew out a breath in response and nudged her for more attention.

Happy he was behind the stall gate, she laughed and gave him a carrot. "And a lover boy, too."

Tori moved on to the next stall to find a pretty bay mare. She gave the horse some attention before she continued her way down the aisle until she reached the corner stall. A small black horse was stood away from the gate and didn't come to greet her.

After another once over, she noticed how thin the animal was. She could see his ribs through his hide, and scars marked his flanks and legs. No doubt he'd been abused.

Tori's chest tightened almost painfully as she opened the gate and slowly stepped inside. The horse reared back his head. She froze on the spot and waited. "Easy, fella." She kept her voice soft and quiet. "I won't hurt you."

Tori took another tentative step and kept her voice low and even. "I'm Tori." She held out her hand and those big brown eyes stared back at her. The horse's distrust made her want to cry. Who would do this to an animal? Her throat burned.

"I just want to be your friend." She was rewarded with a swish of his tail. She had to swallow back the lump in her throat before she could speak again.

"I'll stay right here until you want me to come closer." She pulled a carrot from her pocket and held it out in her palm. "Of course, I'm not past bribing you." After a few seconds, the horse's long neck stretched her way, and finally it took a step closer and retrieved the treat. Tears gathered in her eyes. The single gesture gave her more joy than she'd felt in a long time.

***

Logan walked into the barn. Thanks to his guest, he was already late feeding the horses.

He hoped she would find things in the house on her own and leave him alone. With quick moves, he measured a bucket with oats and headed to his stallion, Ace High.

A nicker sounded and he rubbed the chestnut stallion when it moved into sight.

He rubbed the horse's neck then filled his feeding trough. "Sorry, fella. I got distracted for a little while. Won't happen again."

He couldn't let it. He had to keep his eye on the prize, this land. Of course, now a Slater showing interest in the place could nix his plans.

The two sections he inherited from his grandfather, plus this parcel of land, would be enough for his cattle operation and his horses, and maybe a few crops. The Slaters could keep their homestead, just give up their lease and Logan would be there to claim it. And his dream of raising horses could start coming true.

As he walked toward Buffy's stall, he heard another voice. It was coming from the stall in the corner. Domino. He slowed his steps and stopped when he saw Tori Slater standing with the rescued gelding, rubbing its neck as she spoke soothingly to the animal.

"I can't blame you for not wanting to trust anyone." Her voice was soft, husky quiet as her long fingers stroked over the horse's neck. "I know that feeling. People say they love you, and then, they hurt you."

In sure easy strokes, she continued to rub the horse's coat. "I won't hurt you. No one will ever hurt you again. You're safe here." The animal blew out a breath and bobbed its head.

She smiled, a gesture that lit up her face.

Logan's chest tightened and the feeling went right down into his gut. Damn, if she wasn't seducing that horse. Well, he was immune to women's promises.

As if she sensed his presence, she glanced over at him standing there like a gawking teenager. *Great.* She hadn't trusted him to begin with; now she would think of him as some sort of stalker.

She gave the animal one last stroke and stepped out of the stall while Logan measured out the feed.

"Might not be safe to go into Domino's stall," he told her. "He's been pretty skittish."

Her mouth turned down at the ends. "I would be, too, if someone beat me. Who did this to that poor animal?"

Like hell it was me. "I might do a lot of things, but I don't whip animals. So clear that thought out of your head. I saved him from his abusive owner. Maybe you'll be happy to know the abuser got some jail time. Not enough, but at least Domino is better off."

She relaxed. "I wasn't accusing you. Your other horses are too well cared for. I get angry when anyone raises a hand to creatures or another person who's defenseless."

He had a feeling there was more to her story, but he wouldn't ask. Instead, he nodded to the horse. "I've only had Domino a few weeks. Some people say I should have put him down. But he's a good horse," he spoke quietly. "To see this abuse makes me sick to my stomach. Anyone who puts a hand on defenseless kids or animals is lower than a snake."

Tori could see Logan McNeely's compassion, at least for animals.

"Believe it or not, he's improved a lot since he came here."

"It's nice that you're caring for him."

As he fingered the horse's mane, he nodded. "Nate was the horse rescuer. But even after his passing, people still bring me animals."

His green-eyed gaze met hers. "A few more are out in the pasture, mostly mustangs. The ranchers around here don't like them on their property."

"So, you take in strays?"

"Like I said, my grandfather did, as much as he could afford. With the mustang auction, we'd made enough money for feed and any vet bills. These are the last of them since Nate death, except for Domino." His green eyes locked on hers. "Just so you know, no Slater money was used in the program."

"I didn't ask if it was. I'm sure if my father wouldn't have trusted Nate, he wouldn't have kept him on as manager. I wish I could have met your grandfather." She smiled and her gaze drifted to Domino. "He must have had a special gift to work with wild mustangs."

"He was good with horses. Years ago, he used to train cutting horses."

"What about the cattle operation?" Tori asked.

"In the past few years, your father hasn't cared much about enlarging the herd. He hasn't been to visit here in over three years. We sold off most of the herd last fall after the roundup. The winter was rough and we lost several head." He glanced at her. "Maintaining the herd was all Colt asked of us. We put it all in the ranch books."

Tori didn't know much about accounting. "You and your grandfather did everything fine, and we received the copy of the last cattle sale from your grandfather. That must have been right before he passed away." She paused, hating to bring up bad memories. "My older sister, Ana, and Vance Rivers were named executors about that same time. Since our father had always handled all the ranching affairs, we're just surprised about the operation here."

Logan stopped and stared. "You didn't know about Colton Creek?"

"Not so much. Colt wasn't the type of father to share things with his daughters. Vance Rivers, being Dad's foreman, only knew a little about this place, and nothing about it being the Colton family homestead. I guess you could say my father believed in the need-to-know theory. He finally told us everything when we saw the notice about the land lease coming due."

Something flashed in his eyes, then without a word, he started walking down the aisle. She fell into step alongside him.

"So, would you mind if I came back to visit Domino?"

"Just be careful. I haven't had a chance to work with him."

"Okay, I will."

Eyes wide, he glanced down at her tennis shoes. "Hope you brought along boots and a hat?"

Almost embarrassed, Tori shook her head. She hadn't owned a pair of boots in years. Never needed them living in the city, but she wouldn't mind going riding while she was here. "Can I buy a pair in town?"

He nodded. "First thing tomorrow. This isn't Los Angeles. We protect ourselves with boots and hats for safety."

She paused, searching through their conversation in her mind. "How did you know I was from LA?"

He watched her, his expression unreadable. She wondered if he would answer. Then he said, "The last time your father showed up here, he talked nonstop about his four daughters. The man sounded proud of you all."

The news nearly took her breath away. Was he talking about gruff Colt Slater? The man who hadn't had any time to spend with his daughters when they were growing up?

Summoning great effort, she pushed away the regrets. "I know the difference between Northern Wyoming and Southern California. I might have been away from the ranch for a few years, but I still remember how to handle myself around animals."

She caught the smile twitching at his mouth. "We'll see after I show you around on horseback."

Tori tried not to react. "I don't think that will be necessary."

"Oh, it's definitely necessary. Unless you're too much of a city girl to handle sitting in the saddle for a few hours?"

***

By nine o'clock that evening, Tori was exhausted and already in her pajamas and a sweatshirt for warmth. The spring evening was chilly. She peered out the living room window and saw nothing, except her porch light. The moonless night was really dark.

Note to herself, get security lights.

She turned back to her new home. She had cleaned and tidied enough so she could feel safe eating in the kitchen. Thanks to Logan McNeely she had a bit of food, but tomorrow, she needed to go to town and shop, especially for cleaning supplies.

With her ham sandwich and soup finished, now what? She sighed. She'd worked at the computer and played around with several web design projects, but she wasn't in the mood.

Restlessness filled her and she walked around the large living area. The oversized sofa faced the river rock fireplace, the focal point of the room. The space was cozy, but she still felt uneasy. Maybe because she was in a new place, or that this was the first time she'd been alone since the townhouse in LA.

Here, she was isolated. She couldn't help but wonder if Dane could have somehow found out where she'd gone. No, not possible. If he tried to contact her at the ranch, Colt wouldn't tell him anything. The only people who knew she was here were her sisters, Ana and Josie, and their husbands, Vance and Garrett. And the restraining order forbade him having any contact with her.

Tori walked back to the fireplace and put another log on the fire, then sat on the sofa. Although worn, the cushions were comfortable and she drew the blanket from the ottoman and pulled it over her body. She leaned against the back and closed her eyes. Right now, she didn't want to think any more about the problems in her life, and she had a long list.

Just because her older sisters, Ana and Josie, had gotten married and planned a future didn't mean she had to rush into anything, especially after Dane. At the thought of that man, her chest tightened and she shook her head. No. She wouldn't think about her ex.

Suddenly, a thudding sounded from the side of the cabin. Her body tensed, and then she stood and peeked through the edge of the curtain. She couldn't see a thing, except the swaying of the o a k tree. Probably nothing and she should just go to bed and stop worrying.

Then another thud. Oh, God. Someone was out there. She went to her purse, pulled out her phone and paused. She didn't have Logan McNeely's number. With a sigh, she put down her cell.

Whenever she had a problem, she couldn't run to someone else. She looked around then spotted the coat hooks with a shotgun in the rifle rack. She reached for the old weapon, checked to see if it was in working condition. A bonus, it was also loaded.

She slipped on her jacket, grabbed a flashlight and headed outside. Although she was shaking in her boots, well, in her tennis shoes, she refused to be a victim any longer.

CHAPTER TWO

That evening, Logan walked into the apartment over the barn. The day had been long in more ways than he wanted to count.

He glanced at the old picture of him as a kid with his grandfather on the desk. "Dammit, Pop! I miss you. And right now I could use your advice about our pretty visitor."

Since Nate's death, he hadn't been able to move back to their ranch house. In the bedroom, he removed his boots then stretched out on the double bed. As thoughts of the man who'd raised him flooded his head, he closed his eyes.

After Logan's parents died, Nate McNeely had taken the ten-year-old into his home. And Logan wasn't easy on the old man. He was a kid who'd gotten a bad deal, wanting to strike out at anyone who'd give him the opportunity. Back then, he'd hated just about everything and everyone, including having to leave his home in the city and come to this isolated place.

Logan left for college, and then after graduation, he went into law enforcement in Denver, rarely returning here for visits. Not nearly as often as he should have.

Then one of the worst days of his life happened. A drug bust went terribly wrong. For the second time, his grandfather rescued him, scooping up the broken man and bringing him back to the ranch to heal.

Three years of hard work helped him come back from the hell he'd tried to sink into. But Nate hadn't let him. Logan rubbed his side. The old wound hurt only enough to remind him of his past, a past that caused him more than physical scars, and reminded him of the mistakes he'd made and couldn't change. Of the people he couldn't save.

He covered his eyes with his arm, pushing aside the picture of the night that haunted him still three years later.

Returning here and working with the horses had been therapeutic. The job gave him a focus which was so much better than dealing with people, or relationships. Now, Nate was gone and Logan was truly alone.

His thoughts turned to Tori Slater. He'd known her type. Privileged. No doubt she'd gotten everything handed to her. Now she was here, intruding on his dream to own his own place, interrupting his solitude. He rolled over on his side. He couldn't let her do that.

Suddenly, a shot rang out into the night. "What the…" Muscles tensed, he jumped up and pulled on his boots, grabbed his coat and rifle off the rack. He raced out the door and headed toward the cabin. Then he saw her standing on the porch, silhouetted by the light spilling from the open door. Thank God, she was safe.

"Tori," he called.

She swung and pointed the shotgun at him.

"Whoa, it's me, Logan." He raised a hand in surrender. "How about you put down the weapon."

Her shoulders drooping, she did as he asked.

With slow steps, he walked close. "What the hell happened?"

Even in the dim light, she looked pale. He took the shotgun from her shaky hands and leaned it against the post along with his.

"Someone was outside the cabin." She sighed and sagged against him.

"I'll check as soon as I get you inside. Can you walk?"

Her breath puffed out and she straightened. "Of course I can walk," she told him.

He could see she was shaken. He didn't let her go as he pushed opened the door and felt her softness sagged against him. With an arm around her waist, he helped her inside and directed her to the sofa, then reached over and turned on a light on the table.

She blinked at him. "Sorry, I didn't mean to disturb you." She tried to stand.

Pressing a hand on her shoulder, he stopped her. "You should stay put until your color comes back."

He sat on the ottoman in front of her and glanced around at the clean room. She'd been busy in the past few hours. He was more concerned about what she actually heard that frightened her so much.

"What did you see out there?"

She shook her head. "There was something or someone beside the cabin," she told him.

"Well, the safest thing was to stay in the cabin," he offered. "And the next time before you go out shooting in the dark, call me first. You could have tangled with a mountain lion."

Her midnight gaze searched his face. "A what?"

"We have big cats in the area. They don't usually come near the houses, but you never know. We lost a calf a few weeks ago."

"I shot at a mountain lion?"

Why did he get the feeling she was more worried about her target being a human predator. "More like a raccoon or a coyote."

His gaze strayed from her face, and he realized she wore a pair of pajamas bottoms and a tank top under her unzipped sweatshirt. He glanced away from temptation of the outline of her hard nipples against the thin material. In a rush, he stood. Damn, he'd been alone too long. Time to go.

"I think you scared off whatever it was. I'll look around when I leave. Just stay inside tonight and you should be okay."

"You're leaving?" She rose and followed him.

He stopped at the door, refusing to think her invitation to stay was anything more than just her fear talking. He turned and looked in those incredible eyes. "We all need sleep."

"It's early," she told him. "Why not stay and... have a cup of hot chocolate? You can tell me more about the ranch."

"Because some of us have to get up at dawn and do chores."

She folded her arms under her breasts.

A move that didn't help his situation.

"I could help you."

He frowned. "How many hours have you spent in a saddle?"

"Plenty. When I was teenager I helped with roundup. I rode a lot, though lately not so much. Do you have a lot of chores?"

She walked into the kitchen area, and opened the refrigerator for milk. After pouring the liquid in a pan, she placed it on the gas stove and turned on the heat.

Three long strides brought him to the counter. "I need to check the herd. It's calving season."

Looking over her shoulder, she smiled at him and his gut tightened. Dammit.

She turned to the cupboard, raised up on the balls of her feet and pulled down two mugs and a box of powdered cocoa.

As his gaze went to her shapely bottom, he nearly groaned.

She began scooping in two teaspoons of chocolate powder. “How many calves are you expecting to drop this spring?”

“Hard to say. Couple dozen.” Was this a quiz?

“The Lazy S operation used to have two or three hundred in the spring. My sisters and I used to ride out to find them. Hereford calves have that cute white face. Of course, rule was, we couldn’t name them. Colt would never allow that.”

“Wise man. Steers aren’t pets.”

With care, she poured the steaming liquid into the mugs and handed him one.

He looked at her a moment, then took what she offered. Suddenly he tried to think back to the last time he drank cocoa. He took a sip of the rich brew, and Tori did the same as she leaned against the old butcher-block counter.

“May I ask why there aren’t any security lights?”

“We have them in the barn, but never saw any reason for here. It’s been years since anyone has lived in this house. The last time I saw Colt was nearly three years ago and he stayed in the bunkhouse.”

“Did he seem worried about this operation?”

Logan wasn’t sure. “He spent most of the time with Nate. My grandfather said they weren’t going to do anything different.”

"The Colton Creek hasn't been profitable in a while. The land lease is coming due, and the family has to make some changes."

He couldn't seem to take a breath then he managed, "Colt's letting the lease expire?"

Her gaze flickered from the counter to the light fixture. "Like I said earlier, there have been a lot of things that have happened lately. Dad's stroke for one. And your grandfather ran this place for years, now he's gone."

His body stiffened. "You saying you don't like how I've been doing the job?"

She shook her head. "No, I'm just saying that my family has to make some decisions. How we can start making this place pay for itself again. Vance is married to my sister, Ana, and he still runs the Lazy S so neither one wants to be this far away from Montana. The situation's the same with Josie, she married last month and Garrett owns a construction business in town."

"What about you?" That was a crazy question.

She shrugged. "I came here because it was my turn to help out the family. I guess I need to buck up and stop jumping at every sound I hear."

He studied her from over his mug. "Some people just aren't cut out for this kind of life."

She didn't comment, just sipped her cocoa and he noticed how pretty her olive skin was, all creamy and soft. He'd heard rumors Colt's wife was Hispanic. If so, this daughter had inherited her mother's sultry ebony eyes. The beautiful package wasn't helping his concentration.

Tori shook her head. “I’m not usually like this. I don’t go running into the night shooting at... nothing.”

He could see she’d been pretty shaken. The cop in him had to ask, “What are you *usually* like?”

She smiled, a true smile that crinkled the skin around her eyes.

The gesture hit the target as his body stirred with desire.

“I wouldn’t make a scene if my life depended on it. That’s more my twin’s thing. Josie is the Attention-getter in the family.” Tori’s mouth tightened. “I had a rough few months. Then this trip came up, and there was no one else available, so I volunteered. My two sisters are newlyweds. Don’t get me wrong... I’m glad they’re both happily married, but even seeing that much joy can get on a person’s nerves.”

The next question was all personal, but that didn’t stop him. “There’s no man in your life?”

He watched her eyes widen, not in surprise but fear.

“No.” She shook her head. “Right now, my concentration is on my web design business and this place.”

Okay, she didn’t want to talk about it, neither did he. “So, you thought a little solitude would help.”

“I was hoping coming here would help me regroup. And here I have trouble getting through my first night.” She looked at him. “I apologize.”

"No need." He shook his head, then picked up the pen on the counter and wrote down his cell number. "Next time, call me."

Fingers clasping the paper, she smiled.

Logan felt a little rousing deep in his gut. Definitely time to go.

"Here's mine." She wrote down her cell phone number, too.

He stuffed the paper into his shirt pocket. "I better call it a night. Like I said, five AM comes early."

She walked him to the door. "I promise I won't disturb you again tonight."

He nodded and left. Too late, this woman was bound to cause him many a sleepless night.

***

The next morning, Tori felt refreshed and ready to start her day. She cooked bacon and eggs, wishing she could share the meal with someone. Her thoughts turned to Logan. She was a little embarrassed that she practically talked his ear off last night. What had gotten into her? She'd planned to come here and hole up in the cabin. Alone.

She took her coffee and walked outside to enjoy the sunshine. The temperature was unusually warm for March, so she was going to take advantage of this good weather. LA had perfect weather, but too many bad things had happened to her there. Things she wanted to forget.

So what did she do? First day, she'd tried to keep the good-looking caretaker captive. And he put up with her erratic behavior. Logan McNeely had been kind enough to listen to her ramblings and not laugh at her fears. Too bad she wasn't interested in a relationship with a good-looking cowboy. This was time for work, work, and more work for her.

Her cell phone rang. She went back inside and glanced at the screen to spot her twin sister's name. "Hey, I thought you were on your honeymoon?"

Josie laughed. "We came home early. So how is it going in Wyoming?"

"The place is very beautiful and a little isolated, but that's ranch life." Then she went on to explain about Nate McNeely's death and that his grandson had taken over the operation.

Josie asked, "The important question is, are you comfortable staying there?"

Tori thought back to last night and shuddered. "I still jump at noises. And I hate Dane for making me feel that way."

"Well, don't even think about Mr. Buckley. He's out of your life and he has no idea where you are. There is good news, even though Dane can't be charged for destroying the townhouse, Detective Brandon said he hasn't left LA in weeks. So he hasn't been looking for you."

She clenched the phone tighter. "Wish I had pressed charges when I had the chance."

"You have the restraining order. Besides, we can't go backwards, sis," Josie said. "Speaking of that, I want to talk to you about Colt."

"What happened? Is he okay?"

"Yes. He even went out on horseback yesterday and helped Vance move the herd. I want to ask you to give Dad a chance. He's trying to be the father we always wanted."

Tori was still leery. The men in her life had hurt her, more than loved her. "I'm trying, Josie, but right now I need to think about myself."

"Then you aren't going to like this next bit of news." Josie paused, then said, "Lucia Slater came back to town."

Tori felt the blood pounding in her ears and she had trouble drawing a breath. "Our mother?"

"I wouldn't call her 'our mother', but yes, the woman's back. Colt is the only one who's seen or talked with her. Her story is that she had no choice but to leave us all those years ago that it was to keep us safe."

"And you believe her?" Tori heard the incredulity in her voice.

"No. Garrett is having a private investigator check out the information."

One day, twenty-five years ago their mother up and left her husband and four baby girls. Not long after their father got divorce papers in the mail, and Colt turned away from his daughters.

Tori's stomach clenched. "Do you want me to come home?"

"No, stay put until we get some information. And Tori, I'm sorry. I hated to pile on bad news."

Tori rubbed her temple. "It's okay, Josie. I'm glad you didn't keep it from me."

"Like I said, none of us have seen Lucia. Only Dad."

"Okay, call when you hear something."

Josie told her she was forwarding her mail, and then said goodbye.

Tori put her phone back in her pocket. This wasn't how she'd planned to start her day. Of course, she couldn't help but think about the woman who never was a mother to her. She and Josie had been only three years ago when Lucia Delgado Slater left them. Their housekeeper, Kathleen had been the one to fill that void, had been the only mother Tori knew. How could she welcome this stranger when she'd never been in her life?

Tori looked down at the rotting boards in the porch. She needed to stay busy and what better place to start? Besides, weak boards were a safety issue. She'd have to go into town, but first she'd find Logan and see if he needed anything.

Remembering last night, she hesitated. What had possessed her to spill her guts? She barely knew the man. Odd that she'd felt comfortable talking with him.

She got her denim jacket and headed toward the barn. Before long she spotted Logan in the corral. He was working a dapple gray mustang in the arena chasing a yearling calf. The precision of the equine's moments were remarkable. Yet, she was more interested watching the man.

Logan McNeely sat in the saddle as if born to it. His black Stetson was pulled low over his eyes, shadowing his face. This morning his dark stubble was gone.

He held the reins with sure hands and easily led the horse through a series of commands. She knew the cutting horse did most of the work. The rider just sat in the saddle and let the animal do the job he'd been trained for. This man knew what he was doing, too.

Logan saw Tori at the corral railing, but he continued the session until he finished the task. Once Smoky got the calf through the gate he patted the gelding's neck praising him for a job well done.

"Good boy, Smoky." He wheeled the animal around and rode toward the other side of the corral and stopped in front of Tori.

"Good morning," she greeted him.

He leaned his arms against the saddle horn. "That was hours ago. It's nearly ten now."

She used her hand to shade her face from the sun. "I guess I lost track of time. How busy is your day?"

"Why? You still want to help?"

"If you need me," she said. "But I was going into town and wondered if you want to go, or if not, can I bring you back anything?"

"Are you going to buy some boots and a hat?"

Why was he so worried about her attire? Her shoulders tensed. "Among other things."

He nodded and swung down off the horse. "Give me twenty minutes."

She climbed through the railing and caught up with him. "What's his name?"

"Smoky."

She smiled and began petting the horse as they strolled across the corral. "Nice animal. Is he one of your grandfather's rescues?"

"Yeah. He showed a lot of promise as a cutter." Logan led the horse into the cool barn and into a stall.

"Would you mind if I visited Domino while you take care of Smoky?"

Logan hesitated then nodded. "Be careful," he warned and watched her walk off. She had on a pair of jeans the showed off the gentle sway of her hips. For a small girl, Tori Slater had plenty of curves to get a man's attention. Great. Now he'd let her distract him. Again. He removed the tack from the horse, and then began wiping him down.

He didn't need to get chummy with the person who could keep him from having his own place. He reached for the brush and ran long sure strokes along the horse's flank.

With a shake of his head, Smoky let him know that he liked the attention. That made Logan smile. Okay, so maybe lately he'd been getting along better with animals than people.

Once finished with the chore, he went to see what his visitor was up to. She was still in Domino's stall, stroking the animal's neck and chattering away. He could see the animal enjoyed her interest. What's not to like about a pretty sweet-talking woman?

He got close enough to hear some of the conversation. "I'm sorry you were hurt. I bet you loved him, too." The horse bobbed its head, but she didn't move away. "Well, you don't need to worry, Domino, because you're safe now." She hugged the animal's neck, laying her head against his coat. Although the horse was not large, Tori looked tiny next to its side. "You have a good home now. You don't have to be afraid anymore. I know that's hard to believe. It's hard for me, too. I'm just like you, I trusted someone…" He words trailed off.

Someone hurt her? Like physically? Logan stiffened. Was that why she overreacted last night?

"But we're lucky," Tori told the gelding as she fingered its mane. "We both are in a safe place now."

CHAPTER THREE

Thirty minutes later, Tori was seated next to Logan in his older crew-cab pickup and headed for Dawson Springs. She glanced across the seat to the man who was a puzzle. She wasn't the best judge of character, not with her lousy track record with the men in her life. They'd all been far from perfect. Her father was at the top of the list.

And what did she know about Logan McNeely? Only that his grandfather had been the caretaker of Colton Creek Ranch.

She turned her attention out the window to the beautiful mountain views. She released a breath, feeling a rush of excitement on seeing the untouched land, the wide open spaces, and miles of open pastures. Her thoughts went to her great-great-grandmother Rachel and could imagine her taking this trip into town in a wagon.

"How long has the town of Dawson Springs been here?"

"Since eighteen-ninety-two. It still isn't much in the town, but you can drive to Cody if you need to shop." He glanced at her and raised an eyebrow. "Of course, everyone shops on the internet now."

Tori suddenly realized how isolated they were out here. "That option does make things convenient, doesn't it? You can buy whatever you want, any time day or night."

She watched how easily his large hands commanded the steering wheel as he drove along the two-lane road. She also remembered how gentle his touch had been last night. She hated that she was still so leery of any man. Would it ever go away? "I'm usually working at all hours of the night."

"When the creative mood strikes you?"

"Usually because I can't get everything finished during the day."

He shook his head. "Well, you shouldn't have any distractions here. I'll stay out of your way."

She didn't want him to completely disappear. "Although I plan to work on my design business, I also want to learn about this area and my family's history here." With her own eyes, she needed to see what was required to make this place profitable. Was there room in this area to open the ranch to anglers, or maybe a guest retreat?

"So Colt is serious about making changes?"

"We have to start doing things differently or we could lose everything." She had been the one who'd volunteered to come here, so she was taking this job seriously. "Colt let a lot of things slide the last few years. There were financial reasons, and his stroke. Without money, he couldn't reinvest in the ranch. The Lazy S was in similar shape and my older sister, Ana, and her husband Vance, started renting cabins to anglers." Why was she telling him all this? "That's when she discovered problems here." She glanced at his strong profile. "I wish you'd have told us."

Logan gripped the wheel tighter, trying to stay composed. "What was there to tell? My grandfather made a lot of suggestions, but your father always said, 'I'll think about it.' We just thought the reason nothing happened was because running two ranches was too much trouble."

He stole a glance sideways. "There were good years when Colt and Nate ran a large herd of Hereford mix. My grandfather told me how Colt visited more often back then, even had to hire extra men for roundups. Then about eight or nine years ago, he stopped coming here so often."

Tori frowned. "That was about the same time Josie and I moved to Los Angeles. Our younger sister, Marissa, went away to college."

Logan had left here for a law enforcement career in Denver. So both older men had lost their families. He had moved away by then, too.

His grandfather's job had been reduced to only a caretaker. That's when he started working with the mustangs, and concentrating on his own herd.

With Colt's lack of interest in the homestead, he and his grandfather had hoped to pick up the sections of leased land that Colt held title on. The Colton Creek Ranch would still be left with good acreage.

She sighed and leaned her elbow on the window. "I can't believe Colt let our ancestor's home just fall into ruin. I know it's a ways from the Lazy S in Montana, but this place is our history."

Here was the million dollar question. Logan took a deep breath before asking. "So what are your plans for it?"

"I definitely want to make repairs to the cabin, starting with the front porch. Do you have some time? I'll pay you for the work, of course."

He shook his head. "You already pay me. I just wasn't sure what you wanted done to the place. Nate asked Colt, but he said he'd get to it."

"Repairs are not your responsibility. You're only paid for the job as caretaker, and Ana emailed me this morning to let me know you haven't been paid in months. And your salary wasn't much to begin with. We need to correct that."

"The salary is so low because my grandfather and I worked out an exchange deal with Colt to use grazing land to run our own herd."

"Was that your cattle herd I saw yesterday?"

He nodded. "The herds are grazing together only because of the roundup." When the town came into view, he was suddenly glad. "When my grandfather passed away, I couldn't keep them separated, but they're branded--yours with a double C, and mine with MC."

She frowned. "What about the calves?"

Clever woman. She was definitely a rancher's daughter. "We'll have to wait and see how many drop and then divide them."

"I guess it's the only solution. In the future, we'll have to think of a better system."

"If you want, you can ride out and separate them yourself." He parked in front of the general store and yanked out the keys. "Always worked for your dad." He climbed out and stormed off, leaving her there. Too many other things needed doing than worrying about a woman who wanted to play boss.

He heard his name called. Dammit. Hands on hips, he stopped, but didn't turn around. He took a few breaths as the petite woman stepped in front of him.

"I apologize, Logan. I never meant to suggest... to accuse you of anything. You and your grandfather did an outstanding job keeping up the barn and outbuildings, doing far more than was asked. I only meant that the cattle running together might not be fair... to you."

He finally looked at her. "My grandfather might not have gotten much into my head as a kid, but one of the things I learned was I don't take what isn't mine. Cattle rustling is about as low as a person can get."

Her ebony eyes met his gaze. Her face was so pretty, her mouth so tempting. "I can think of a few things lower," she whispered then straightened. "I can't ask you to do a job when you don't have any help."

He didn't need Tori Slater to hang around to help, or to go shooting off the shotgun late at night and practically falling in his arms. He couldn't let her mess up everything. And he wasn't only thinking about the land. "Be careful what you volunteer for."

"I've been told that before." She tossed him a wide smile.

His gut clenched, making him realize how long it had been since he had time for a woman. Just not this woman. Maybe if he was lucky she'd get bored soon and go back to where she came from.

"Well, if you're gonna play cowgirl you need the right equipment."

"It's been a few years since I've worn a pair of western boots. I guess I could use a little help in deciding what's best."

He turned and started down the sidewalk. "Just be warned, Clara Williams will probably ask you a lot of questions."

She stepped in beside him. "Well, I'm hoping I have the answers."

"If you want to know anything about the history of the town and the area, she's the one to ask. Just don't tell her any secrets."

He saw something flash across her face. Sadness.

"Maybe that's a little strong. Clara is really nice; she's been a good friend to me and Nate." He started to reach out to touch her, but stopped himself. "Come on, we've got a lot to do today."

He reached for the door handle and held it open, allowing her to step inside the huge storefront building, Williams General Store. The walls were lined with shelves stacked with jeans. The boot section was on the other wall, where boxes filled those shelves. There were round racks of women's blouses and jackets and one for men's shirts.

"Logan," a woman's voice called out.

He turned to see the attractive middle-aged woman coming toward them. She was tall and slender and wore her standard uniform, a Western-cut blouse, a pair of jeans and boots. Her hair was honey blond and had a few streaks of gray. Tiny lines circled her kind hazel eyes.

"Hi, Clara."

"What brings you into town during the week?"

"I brought in Tori Slater so you can meet her, and she needs some practical clothes."

Tori stepped forward. "Hello, Clara. It's nice to meet you. And thank you for the sheets and towels. That was something I didn't think to bring with me."

"You're welcome." Clara studied her. "I can see a resemblance to your father. I hope Colt is well."

"He is now. He had a stroke a few months back, but he's been lucky and has nearly made a total recovery."

"A stroke?" She glanced at Logan, her lips pinched tight. "I had no idea."

Over the years, Clara had kept up on all the news in the area. She'd known Colt Slater, and probably a lot about Rachael Colton's family. Logan wondered if something might have gone on between Clara and Colt. Why not? They were both consenting adults.

"Well, give him my best." She smiled. "What exactly can I help you with today?"

"I could use a pair of boots," Tori said.

Clara escorted them over to the shoe section and then started bringing out different styles. Finally after about thirty minutes, Tori decided on a pair of lace up brown Ropers. Then she picked out two pairs of jeans and two blouses. The hard part for Logan was being distracted as she came out of the dressing room modeling her selections.

"Well, if you don't look like you're ready for riding the range," Clara said as Tori stood in front of the full-length mirror in stone-washed jeans that hugged her curves. A wine-colored long sleeve Henley T-shirt fit snug against her breasts and small waist.

Okay, he wouldn't get much sleep tonight. Again.

"I plan to do a lot of cleaning and some repairs," Tori told Clara.

"The cabin has been closed up so long."

Tori arched an eyebrow. “You’ve been out there?”

Logan swore he saw a blush across Clara’s face. “It’s been years,” the older woman said. “And it’s been a long time since Colt came here.” She quickly changed the subject. “Do you have plans for the place?”

Tori glanced at Logan. “I’m not sure. We’re just making some a few repairs for now. The structure is well over a hundred years old.”

“It’s built well. They don’t make them like that anymore.”

After deciding to wear one of her new outfits home, she paid for the purchases at the cash register. Then they said their goodbyes and walked out.

Logan opened Tori’s door, then he climbed in behind the wheel and drove to the end of town to Watson’s Lumberyard. He shut off the engine, and started to get out, but Tori reached across the seat and touched his arm.

“I don’t know Clara, but did she act like she wasn’t telling us something?”

He shrugged, debating about revealing his suspicions.

“Do you know something?”

“I can’t say for sure, but I think at one time, she and Colt might have been friends… good friends.”

Confusion filled Tori’s thoughts as her eyes widened. Dear old Dad. She smiled. “Oh, boy, can’t wait to tell my sister this news.”

Tori saw the curious look on Logan's face, and she went on to explain. "Our father has had a pretty miserable disposition ever since our mother left all those years ago. He pretty much ignored us girls." She sighed. "Since his stroke he's been trying to change and build a relationship with us."

"How do you feel about him now?"

"I'm not sure if I can do the father-daughter thing. But it's nice to know he was human, and he had needs."

"Is that the reason you came to Wyoming? To get away from him."

Tori froze. She didn't want to tell anyone her past. "I just returned from LA to help with my father's care. When we learned this homestead existed, it was my turn to help out." She had nothing to keep her there, but she didn't want to spread that information around.

"Are you planning to go back to LA?"

Tori shook her head, not wanting to think about that time in her life when she'd been a fool over the wrong man. She had plenty of reminders of her mistakes, her fears.

"No, I shared office space with Josie. Now that she's moved to Montana permanently, there's no reason for me to return to California. I'm lucky I can run my design business anywhere."

He gave her an odd look, but she wasn't about to say any more. "Speaking of business, I think we better get that wood for the repairs."

He climbed out and shut the door.

Thoughts racing, she met him at the door to the store. Did he know she was hiding her true reason for being in Wyoming?

Logan gave the clerk the order for the materials needed for the porch. Then he leaned a hip against the counter and looked at her. "If you want to do it right, you should replace the rotted posts. Then you don't have to worry about replacing them in a few years."

She had some money of her own to pay for it. Suddenly, redoing Rachel's place was important. "Yes, let's do it right. After all, it's my family's home." And hers for now.

***

After arranging for the lumber to be delivered the next morning, they stopped by Hansen's Market for more groceries. Another detour was a quick lunch at the local hamburger place, then Logan headed out of town. The drive back to the ranch was quiet, but he liked it that way. He'd never been much of a talker, especially since he spent most days alone.

About a mile from the ranch, Logan surprised himself when he said, "If you aren't busy this afternoon, I'm moving the herd. Would you like to ride along?"

He glanced across the cab and saw the twinkle in her eyes. "Really, you want me along?"

"This is your ranch, your cattle. Well, part your cattle." He watched her indecision, and then added, "Unless you think you can't keep up."

"Whoa, cowboy. Those are fightin' words. I'm a fourth generation rancher and have been sitting in a saddle since I was five years old."

He readjusted his hat to hide his smile. "So I take it that's a yes."

She gave him a curt nod.

Twenty minutes later, Tori showed up in the corral as he led both Smoky and a chestnut mare, Buffy, out of the barn.

Seeing her smile, he found he was looking forward to the ride for a change. Oh, boy, he'd been alone too long.

"Oh, I get to ride Buffy." She immediately went to the animal. "She's a beautiful horse."

Buffy bobbed her head as if agreeing.

"She's a good mount around cows. Climb on and I'll adjust your stirrups." Cupping his hands, he offered her a leg up, and as she easily swung up into the saddle, he caught a whiff of her citrus scent. He tried to stay detached, but this woman pushed all his buttons.

He shook off the distraction and did his job. "How's that?"

Moving her feet, she tested them. "Perfect." She pushed her straw cowboy hat more securely on her head. It shaded her face now. But he didn't miss the excitement in her dark eyes.

With reins in hand, he grabbed Smoky's saddle horn, put his boot into the stirrup, and swung his leg over the animal's back.

He wheeled the gelding around and watched Tori. She walked Buffy around the corral as he examined both her and her horse closely, how well she handled the animal. She looked good in the saddle.

"Okay, let's go."

As he led her out of the corral, he checked his watch. He hoped that his friend, Seth, would show up to help. He had texted him, letting him know he could use a hand with the herd.

Within a few minutes, he got her on the trail; then they cut across the pasture toward the herd. It was springtime so he could move the mama and calf operation to high ground and fresh grass.

After seeing where Logan headed, Tori guided her horse beside him. She hadn't ridden in so long it felt good to take the time to enjoy the peace and quiet. She looked around. My Lord, this place was beautiful. She studied the mountain's unique rock formation dotted with pine trees deep within the crevices.

Enjoying the easy movement of the horse Tori asked, "How long has it been since any crops were planted?" She had noticed an equipment barn a ways back.

"Long time, since I was a kid," Logan said, with a wave. "I'd been prepping the south section to plant wheat, but then Grandpa got sick."

"May I ask what was wrong with him?"

"Lung cancer. He'd smoked for years and I finally got him to quit, but it was already too late. He didn't want any treatment either." The gentle sway of the horses was soothing, but she could see his sorrow. "He died here where he wanted to be."

Tori quickly wiped away a tear. "I'm sorry. I wish I could have met him."

"Yeah, he was an ornery old cuss. But I miss him." Logan shook his head. "If you're lucky enough to have a second chance with your father, I'd say take it. You don't want to have any regrets."

Emotions clogged her throat and she could only nod, reminded of how her father looked after she'd seen him after his stroke. Although Colt was nearly back to a hundred percent physically, his strong, stubborn spirit had taken a big hit. She'd recalled seeing the vulnerability in his blue eyes.

She also remembered how he reached out. Could he really change? Did he really want her in his life?

Tori tried to concentrate on the miles of open pasture covered by new grass, and the sound of the stream. Colton Creek was brimming with the spring runoff. The fishing was probably very good here.

Logan scanned the range and shifted in the saddle. He never liked to share things, but this woman had him chatting away. Their conversations needed to be about business and only business. His job was to talk her out of wanting to enlarge the operation here. He didn't want any personal stuff between them when he walked away with her land.

He spotted the herd and immediately wondered what Tori would think. It was small, only about seventy head, maybe two dozen calves. He wanted to run more, a lot more head.

If he put out Ace for stud, he could use the money to buy another breeding bull and increase the herd. Right now, everything was on hold until he knew what the Slaters were going to do.

"There they are."

Logan kicked his heels into Smoky's flanks and the horse shot off across the pasture. He needed to feel the cool breeze against his face, the freedom of the open spaces and blue sky. He'd taken over thirty years to learn the truth, but he found this was what he loved to do.

He felt Tori's presence before he saw her. A quick glance and he found she was catching up. The lady could ride. He slowed when they reached the herd. That was when he spotted his neighbor coming from the other direction.

Seth Cameron was about his age, but the similarities stopped there. He'd been married, built a house and had a small rodeo rough stock business. Then two years ago, his world fell apart when his wife and child were killed in a freak car accident.

That was the start of a tough time for Seth, with drinking and other destructive behavior. Logan felt the man deserved the right to grieve, but when things had turned dangerous, he'd stepped in to help his friend. Recently, Seth seemed more like his old self.

The tall man was on his large black gelding racing across the field, and then as he neared them, he pulled back on the reins to make a quick stop.

"Hey, Logan, I got your SOS."

"Sorry about the short notice. I appreciate you coming to help."

"What are friends for?"

His neighbor glanced toward Tori, so Logan did the introductions. "Tori Slater, this is our neighbor and my friend, Seth Cameron. Seth, this is Tori Slater."

"A pleasure to meet you, Tori." He gave her a smile as his fingers touched his hat. "So you're Colt's daughter. Did he send you to check up on this guy?"

Tori smiled and leaned forward on the pommel. "Why, do I need to?"

That caused Seth to laugh.

It was good to see his friend back to the easy-going guy Logan remembered, although he was surprised by his downright flirting.

"We better get started," Logan directed them to the herd. "We're losing daylight."

Seth untied his lariat from his saddle. "I'm ready." He looked at Tori and grinned. "Come on, I'll show you how it's done here in Wyoming."

"I already know my way around cattle. Remember, I'm Colt Slater's daughter."

Seth smiled again.

A gesture that irritated Logan, and his fingers tensed on the reins. "From what I hear, there are three more of you ladies back in Montana."

"Yes, there are. We run that ranch, too."

Logan wasn't sure what that meant. Would she stay and take over Colton Creek? He thought back to her trouble last night just staying alone in the cabin. Could she last here?

In no time, the threesome reached the herd. The day was cool enough, but the cattle didn't want to go anywhere. The calves were bawling and spooked easily. Seth jumped at the chance to run them down and bring them back. The next time one shot off, his friend coaxed Tori into bringing it back.

Great. Now, he had to listen to the laughter and banter between the two.

By the time the job was finished, the sun was heading down in the western sky. "It's time to call it a day."

Seth nodded, then tipped his hat. "It's been a pleasure, Miss Slater. Hope to see you again."

"Thank you, Mr. Cameron. And thank you for your help today."

"Call me any time. See you later, Logan."

Logan nodded and thanked him, but he found he wasn't happy about how the day turned out. He shouldn't care what happened between those two. His back straightened. Then why in the hell did he?

***

The next morning, Tori woke and rolled over in bed. Unlike the previous night, she'd managed eight full hours of sleep, even with all the creaks and moans of the old cabin. For the most part, the aches and pains from being in the saddle over four hours yesterday hadn't even bothered her.

She sat up in the four-poster bed with the incredibly soft feather mattress and gazed around. Had her great-great-grandmother slept in this room? Had her babies in this bed?

Last night, after a long soak in the old claw-foot tub to help her muscle soreness, she'd found an old cedar chest. Inside were pictures and old letters. Fatigue hit hard and she'd decided she needed some sleep and would go through things today.

She sat on the edge of the mattress and stretched, then went to the window and looked out. The sun was bright and shining on the mountains. The pine and rock-covered peaks looked beautiful with the brilliant blue sky as the backdrop.

She'd always loved the view at the Lazy S, but coming here to Wyoming, especially after yesterday's ride, had made her curious. This was the place that the family legacy started. She was anxious to find out more about her family and how they'd come to settle here.

She started to back away when she noticed Logan coming out of the barn. The man's strides were long but easy. His body was lean, framed by his massive shoulders and covered with a denim jacket. If she let herself she could strike up some interest in the man without the least bit of a struggle. But she didn't trust herself.

Logan slowly raised his head and saw her in the second-story window. As his finger touched the brim of his hat in greeting, her pulse did a little dance. She struggled to pull on the wooden window sash, and it finally gave way. "Good morning," she called out in the cool morning air.

"Mornin'. The lumber was delivered and I'm about to start on the porch, but I didn't want to wake you."

She glanced at the clock. Oh, dear, the time was after nine o'clock. "I'm up now. I'll be down to help as soon as I get dressed."

She quickly went through her morning routine and dressed in her new jeans and boots, which she'd broken in by wearing them all day yesterday. She slipped on a long sleeved Henley over a tank top. She pulled her hair into a ponytail and went downstairs, and unlocked the front door and found that Logan had already taken out the rotted wood and tossed it into a pile on the lawn. Sawhorses with a sheet of plywood made up a table for his saw.

She carefully walked across the remaining floor beam to get to the yard. "You've been busy," she told him, wondering why he seemed to be less friendly this morning.

"You need a porch, so it'll get done." He studied what was underneath the rotten wood. "This frame was in worse shape than I first thought. We need to pour new fittings to secure the frame. So I went into town earlier to get extra material."

He had been busy. Guilt sliced through her over sleeping so late. "Just make sure you give me the bill. What can I do?"

"I've already dug the new footings, so I'm ready to mix the concrete. If you have some coffee, I wouldn't mind a cup."

She nodded and started her cautious trip across to the door when he called.

"I stopped by the post office." He went to the work table and picked up a priority envelope and handed it to her. "This is for you."

She glanced at the familiar Montana return address. "Ana sent me my mail." She stepped inside the doorway, tore open the large envelope and began sorting through the letters, bills and advertisements, but then came to a plain white envelope. Her breath caught when she saw it was addressed to Vicki Slater. Her heart stopped. Oh, God, no.

Logan peered through the open door to ask a question when he caught the panicked look on Tori's face.

That look propelled him inside. "Is something wrong? Is it Colt?"

She released a slow breath and brushed back her hair with a shaky hand. "No. Everything is fine." She turned away to fill the coffeepot.

He didn't believe her. He walked across the cabin and to the counter. He glanced down at the stack of mail to see an envelope addressed to Vicki Slater with no return address.

"They call you Vicki?"

He watched her back stiffen at the mention of the name. His old cop instincts kicked in. She was terrified of something… someone. "Who, Tori? Who is this guy?"

She turned, her face laced with fear. She blew out a breath. "He wasn't supposed to find me. I thought I would be safe here."

CHAPTER FOUR

Safe? Who was she running from?

Seeing Tori's distress, Logan went to her and reached out, but stopped short of touching her. "Who wasn't supposed to find you?"

She quickly came out of her daze and shook her head. "It doesn't matter."

The hell it didn't. He took the envelope from her and read the name. "Vicki Slater."

Her eyes widened. "Don't call me that. My name is Tori."

He raised a soothing hand, then slowly lowered it. "Hey, you okay?"

She brushed back her hair. "Sure, I'm fine." She forced a smile. "I couldn't be better."

Seeing her tremble, he didn't believe her. Whoever wrote this letter had her terrified. "Doesn't look that way to me."

"It was a surprise," she insisted. "I wasn't expecting to hear from this person." She stepped back. "Hey, weren't you going to mix some cement?"

"Concrete. I'm mixing concrete."

"Then shouldn't we get back to work?"

He wanted to know more, but didn't push it. "You put on the coffee. By then, I'll need you to hold the post while I pour the concrete."

"Okay, give me a few minutes."

Tori put on her best brave face and hoped Logan would drop the issue. Their gazes held for several seconds. She released a shaky breath when he finally turned and walked back outside.

She finished making coffee then eyed the letter on the counter as if it were something deadly. To her, it was.

Dane had found her. That was the worst that could happen. She picked up her phone and punched in Josie's number.

Her sister answered right away. "Hey, Tori. How's it going?"

"Perfect until this morning when I got the mail you sent. Did you know there was a letter in the package from Dane?"

She heard her twin's quick intake of breath. "Oh, God, no. I would have never sent you something from the bastard."

"I'm sorry. Of course you wouldn't." Her twin had always been very protective of her.

"Okay, what did the jerk have to say?"

She examined the letter and checked the postmark, her stomach turning a flip. "I haven't opened it yet. What I'm really worried about is it was mailed from Butte." That town wasn't far from the Lazy S in Montana.

There was a long silence. "You want me to call Detective Brandon? You can send it to him."

The LA police detective in charge of her case had been as helpful as the law would allow. He'd been there for her restraining order and he also handled the break-in at the townhouse.

She couldn't hold back a sigh. She was really tired of being a victim. She couldn't let Dane have control again.

"I need to see what he has to say first," she told her sister as she carefully opened the envelope. With trembling hands, she unfolded the letter and scanned the typed page.

"Come on, Tori," Josie chimed in. "Read it to me."

"Okay." She began to read out loud.

"Vicki,

Although I miss you, I'm glad you're home with your family. This will give you time to think about us and remember how good it was. Even if people try to keep us apart, you know we belong together. Sooner or later you'll realize the truth, too.

Always, D"

"'You know we belong together'," Josie repeated. "He's sick."

Tori felt a shiver rush through her. She couldn't go through this again. "I need to leave here."

"Wait a minute, Tori. Dane doesn't know you've gone to Wyoming. No one knows where you are except the six of us here. And he's not getting anything from us." Josie paused. "But if you feel better coming back to the Lazy S, of course come home."

Relief washed through Tori, relaxing her a bit. If she went back to Montana, she might cause more trouble for her family. She couldn't forget how Dane destroyed Josie's townhouse. "No, Dane already drove me out of LA. He's not driving me out of my home here."

"Good. So you like it there?"

Tori glanced around the old cabin. The kitchen faucet leaked and the bathroom needed so much help. "I can't explain it, Josie, but I feel a connection here with Rachel Colton. I found her journals, and she wrote about her life settling here all those years ago."

"It's a good thing that you're there?"

"Yes. The cabin is rustic and drafty, but I like it. I can work on my designs, and I can go riding around."

"What about Nate's grandson? Logan? How are things with him?"

Tori glanced out the open door and watched the man in question mixing concrete in a wide bucket. He'd removed his shirt, leaving him in a black T-shirt that molded to his toned body.

She felt a tightening in her stomach, thinking about last night. How he'd showed up and sat with her. "He's fine. He's making some repairs on the cabin that have been long overdue."

"That's good. I know you've only just got there, but have you had a chance to look around? Could this place pay for itself?"

Tori told her sister about her visit to town, and the friendly people, the beautiful landscape. Once again she was distracted by the muscles flexing across Logan's back as he churned the heavy mixture.

"Then don't let this one letter spoil it. I'll put in a call to Detective Brandon and see what he has to say about it."

"Okay. I'll let him look into this." Tori couldn't help but watch the show going on outside the cabin. Logan McNeely was a nice distraction for a change.

Suddenly, he looked up, met her gaze and nodded, indicating he was ready for her. "Hey, Josie, I need to go and help Logan with the porch."

"All right, but if you hear anymore from Dane, call me. You don't have to deal with him alone.

"I will. I promise. Love you. Bye." With a smile, she clicked off the call and shoved her phone into her pocket.

Then Tori hurried outside. "What do you needed me to do?"

"Hold this post plumb while I pour the concrete."

She jumped down into the dirt and stood beside him. The deep holes were dug and the posts were propped inside. Bracing her legs wide, she held the first four-by-four while he poured the mix from the bucket into the hole, then used a level to straighten the post. He was so close she could inhale his scent, a combination of earth, sweat and the man, himself.

"Perfect," he said. "You can let go, but be careful not to knock it."

Over the next thirty minutes, she managed to continue the process until eight posts were seated in the ground and secured with concrete.

He stood back and examined his work. "Looks good. In a few hours, we can start on the frame."

"Good. How about I make you some lunch?"

***

Logan sat at the scarred maple table in the cabin and glanced around. There were so many things he could do to this place to enhance it.

"This cabin had a few additions to the original structure." He stood and walked across the main room to the back wall and examined it closely. "This wall has been pushed out to add on the bathroom and bedroom." He raised his gaze to the staircase and the second floor. "The same with the upstairs."

Tori turned around. "So my great-great-grandparents only lived in this one room?"

He nodded. "A lot of settlers did. They would build the barn first for the livestock while the family lived in the covered wagon. Of course, back then there was an outhouse."

"I'm sure glad somewhere along the line my relatives thought indoor plumbing was a necessity."

"Well, whoever built this cabin did a good job."

"Sounds like you're an expert."

"I majored in architecture my first two years in college."

An eyebrow rose. "I take it you changed."

He nodded, but didn't say any more and she didn't push.

"Well, it's nice to know that my family home is soundly built since I'll be staying here for a while."

Logan tried not to act surprised. Would he have to look after her? "You've decided to stay?"

"My family needs me here." She walked to the table carrying a plate with two grilled cheese sandwiches. She went back to the stove and returned with two mismatched bowls of tomato soup.

He wanted to ask her about the letter, but it was none of his business. Whatever came in the mail earlier still had her a little shaky. A lot more than she'd admit. And he'd bet his best stallion that whoever wrote to her was a guy, an ex boyfriend probably. Someone who'd frightened her badly enough she couldn't talk about it.

Tori sat across from him. "I'm still deciding what to do with the property. I'm thinking the fishing around here has to be pretty good." She picked up her spoon and hesitated. "Trouble is, we don't have any lodging for anglers except this cabin."

He took a bite of his sandwich. "There's a bunkhouse with an apartment on the second floor."

"Would the bunkhouse be suitable to rent out?" She raised a hand. "Aren't you staying in the apartment upstairs?"

"I can move back to the Double M any time." He shrugged. "You should check the place out yourself."

"I will." She put down her spoon. "If we decide to think bigger and turn the place into a guest ranch, we'll need to build some cabins for the visitors. That would be a big financial investment and I'm not sure if the family can handle that right now."

Anglers? Guest ranch? He definitely didn't like any of these plans. He preferred the quiet. The anglers might not be so bad, but city folk running around and on horseback weren't his idea of the best neighbors. "So you don't plan to run cattle any longer?"

"I'm not an expert, but won't building up a herd again take a few years?"

"While you wait, you could plant crops. The land is there, waiting to be used."

"I'm not sure we could afford to pay the men."

He wanted to hope. "You're going to let your land lease go?"

She shrugged. "Like I said, I need to talk to my sisters and Colt. We want to keep the homestead, but we still need to make it work financially. Got any ideas?"

He hesitated, then decided there was no better time to put his cards on the table. "Lots of them, but probably none you'd like."

Lots? Tori wasn't sure she'd heard Logan correctly. What did he want? "Excuse me?"

He pushed back his half-eaten soup. "I'm not crazy about a bunch of city people running around, especially on horseback or worse, four wheelers. Nate and I had planned to increase our herd, but go the natural route with only grass-fed cattle."

She was caught off guard by his announcement. "Really?"

He nodded. "Once the group of new calves dropped this spring and weaned from their mamas, I plan to move them to the new grass in my southern pasture on the Double M. My idea is to raise my yearlings until they're ready to be shipped to market. Grass-fed only, no feed lots with grain laced with hormones, antibiotics or chemicals."

Was she suddenly being abandoned? "You're pulling out of Colton Creek altogether?"

"You mentioned it hasn't been much of a working ranch lately. My grandfather kept it going for years without any interest from your family."

"Like I said before, my sisters and I didn't know about this place. Since we do now, we plan to stay involved."

"You want a *dude* ranch," he said. "I won't help you with that."

"Not a dude ranch, a guest ranch," she emphasized. "Besides, it's only one option I threw out there. Now, you give me some ideas, ones I can work with."

Logan leaned back the chair, balancing on the back legs. The best option would be for her to pack up and go back to Montana and let him win the conflicting bid on the Slater lease. "There are a lot of things you can do, and they're all gonna take work... and money."

She frowned and leaned forward. "Stop thinking I've been pampered all my life because I haven't. Beside tough ranch work, I've been on my own since college—and I worked during those years, too. So show me what you've got and give me a chance, because I'm not walking away from my family homestead."

"You could put in a crop, barley or wheat, or grass for feed. Like you mentioned, Colton Creek has the equipment and it's just sitting there going to ruin." He wouldn't like if they sprayed the lease land with pesticides. "Or you could just stick with cattle."

"What about the idea of allowing anglers on the property? I need fast money to help keep this place, pay the taxes and the lease."

"Are you renting out this cabin, too?" he asked.

Tori glanced around. "I hate the idea that some stranger would be staying here, but will if I have to. It needs work first."

She turned back to him, her dark eyes met his. Damn, he hated the effect just that look had on him.

"I have a proposition for you," she said.

He rested his arms on the table, trying not to think about her asking him for anything other than business. "I'm listening."

"Could you take my share of the new calves from our herd? Raise them on your land along with yours to be grass-fed?"

He tried not to show any reaction. "Like a partnership?"

"Wasn't that what your grandfather and Colt had over the years?"

"No. Nate was the ranch manager for years, then lately, he'd become a caretaker."

She paused a moment, then said, "That doesn't mean we can't be. We can continue with a small herd. I take it you feel safe Colton Creek's pastures have been free of any insecticides."

He nodded. "And over the last two years the herd hasn't been fed any supplements with growth hormones. I've had the Double M certified." *And your lease acreage.* "But this ranch hasn't been tested."

She arched an eyebrow. "Is it fenced?"

"Mostly. I have four months to make it ready."

"If I help you get ready, would you take my calves then?"

"For how long? I have limited acreage."

"Until I can get my pastures tested and certified for organic beef."

He paused. "This isn't a fast fix, Tori. It's taken Nate and me nearly two years to do the prep to grow the grass and legumes." He still wasn't sure he could do this on his own. He'd done nothing but study and read up on the healthy process for beef. They'd kept all pesticides off the Colton Creek lease land on the chance their bid won the lease property.

"If I can make some money with the anglers right away, I can invest in other projects like a beef herd."

She made the process sound like it would be so easy. "Tell me this, what happens when you get bored with this place and go back to LA?"

Tori stiffened. "I'm not going back to Los Angeles, ever. Nothing is left for me there. I'm staying here on the homestead for as long as it takes for the operation to pay for itself. I do like your idea of organic beef and know the asking price is higher. I just need to sell the idea to my family."

She turned that sultry midnight gaze on him and his gut tightened. "And I need to convince you that I'd make a good partner."

Whoa, this was the last thing he wanted. A partnership with this woman. Any woman. He still wasn't sure she wouldn't get bored and decide to leave. But, hell, if she was going to distract him, at least he could make a living while helping her.

"Why don't you talk with your family first?" he suggested. "Your father might not go along with the idea."

"This isn't just Colt's decision. My sisters and their husbands have a vote, too." She got up from the table and reached over the counter. The action caused her jeans to pull over her bottom. Damn, he wasn't going to survive this.

Tori sat again at the table with pen and paper. "I need to write this down to make sure I have everything correct. You've agreed to take my new calves with yours?"

Did he agree to that? "I also plan to increase my herd with seed-stock."

She wrote that down, then said, "So we'll brand my calves. How many mamas and calves are you seeding the herd with?"

"About fifty head," he told her. "This venture is starting slow, Tori. It's won't be fast cash."

She nodded. "I know. If I can start bringing in money from anglers along our river property and put them in the bunkhouse, I should be fine for now." Looking up from her notes, she smiled. "We can use part of that money to help with the fencing and more stock."

She had it all planned out. The plan wasn't his, but it was better than no plan.

"First things first, if you're serious about bringing in anglers, you should talk to Clara," he told her. "She runs a small bait-and-tackle business out of her store. She also knows who comes into town asking about the best fishing spots."

Again, she looked at him and nodded. "Seems we have a lot to do to get started. Would you mind coming up with a starting cost?"

He rambled off things they needed to do with prepping the land, plus seeding and fencing, hoping to scare her off.

Tori just continued to take notes. "Okay, looks like I have enough information to start with"

"Let me know what Colt says. I need to get back to work on the porch." He stood and carried his dishes to the sink before Tori Slater talked him out of anything else. Problem was, part of him wanted to give her whatever she asked for.

***

The next morning, Tori was up at dawn. She showered and dressed, hoping to help Logan finish the porch, so then they could go look at the property along Colton Creek. Good access for the anglers was important, or they could forget about any business venture.

She came downstairs and saw her great-great-grandmother's old cedar chest next to the fireplace. The previous day, she'd dragged it in from the downstairs bedroom so she could have better light to examine the treasures inside. After reading part of Rachel's journal she learned of her great-great grandmother's struggles as she and Cyrus set out to homestead this land.

In the trunk was also a family bible, listing all their children. Rachel had given birth to five babies, three sons and two daughters. A boy, William, died in childbirth along with a daughter, Mary Kathryn, when she was only two-years-old.

Her other daughter, Sarah Millicent, Millie for short, married George Slater from Montana.

By the looks of it, Tori came from pretty tough stock. She was depending on that strength. Did she have what it would take to stay here and start raising cattle? Her thoughts turned to Logan McNeely

Though she had been around this man for two days, she was attracted to the man, yet he was nearly a stranger. But somehow it didn't feel that way. That didn't mean, she would let anything happen between them.

She thought back to Dane and how wonderful he'd been in the beginning. He was so attentive, so sweet to her. Then she made the mistake of moving in with him, wanting to start their life together. Then everything turned bad.

She shook her head and walked into the kitchen where she began to make coffee. Luckily, she'd left that life and the man before he destroyed her future. Was that future here in Wyoming? She smiled, thinking about the ideas for this place running through her head.

"Okay, let's get started." She went to the front door, unbolted the lock and swung it open. She stopped on seeing Logan already at work on the porch.

He was dressed in faded jeans, encasing those long legs. A Henley shirt covered his broad shoulders as he measured for the railing. He looked up at her, his green eyes shaded by the familiar black Stetson. "Morning," he said in a husky voice.

"Good morning." She glanced at the sun coming over the mountain. "You're starting early."

"The animals like to eat about this time, so I thought I'd get this finished, too."

"How about some coffee?"

"I wouldn't turn it down."

She walked back inside and took down two mugs. She had to wait a few more minutes for the coffee. Also the wait gave her time to calm down. Something about seeing Logan McNeely early in the morning felt so… intimate. Just when she started to relax around him, she began to notice he was a good looking man.

"Pull it together," she chided herself as she poured the hot brew into cups, then carried them outside.

The porch floor had been laid yesterday afternoon. She walked off the large temporary step and handed a mug to Logan.

"Thank you," he murmured.

She sat on the edge of the new structure and was surprised when Logan took the space beside her. Neither spoke as she gazed out toward Hart Mountain, snow still covering its peaks. The air was a little cool, but the sun was quickly warming her. A slight breeze rustled the cottonwood trees along the edge of the yard, but did nothing to ease the awareness of the man sitting close by.

She raised a hand toward their view. "This would make a great picture to advertise this place."

"If you're directing your advertising toward anglers, you need to head down to the creek."

"Good idea. I need to have a look anyway and take some pictures to send my sisters."

She liked having projects to keep her busy, and she was anxious to start this one. "As soon as I fix us breakfast, I'll come and help you finish the porch."

He frowned. "You don't need to feed me."

"Let's just say it's payback for another favor."

"What would that be?"

"I bet you know all kinds of good fishing spots along the creek. It would be nice if you could show them to me."

"That's a pretty expensive favor for a breakfast."

She needed this man's help, but more importantly, she trusted him. "What if I throw in a few more meals?"

A twitch of a smile played across his mouth. "What, grilled cheese?"

Thanks to Kathleen, the woman who'd help raise her and her sisters, she could cook. "I could probably come up with something a little more palatable."

He tossed her a rare smile. "I look forward to it."

The fact of how much she was looking forward to spending time with this man surprised her.

CHAPTER FIVE

After lunch, Tori finished up the dishes then went out to the barn to find Logan. He had chores to do first, but offered to show her the bunkhouse later.

She walked through the barn, hoping to see her friend, Domino. But the gelding wasn't in his stall. Had something happened to him?

With quick steps, she went outside to the corral and stopped when she saw the black horse walking behind Logan. She smiled watching the big cowboy's gentleness with the skittish animal.

When Logan spotted her, he motioned for her to join them. She walked into the arena, but knew she couldn't make any sudden moves to spook the horse.

"Hey, Domino," she crooned softly. "Look at you, out and about strolling in the sunshine?"

The horse turned in her direction as she continued toward him and she smiled when he stretched out his head in her direction. She kept her hands low to let the animal see that she wouldn't cause him any harm.

When Domino bobbed his head in greeting, she felt her chest grew tight with emotion. How could anyone hurt this wonderful horse? She was close enough to pet him, her fingers trailing on his bristly coat. "How's my favorite guy?"

Domino pressed his head against her, wanting more attention. "I'm so proud of you coming out here."

After giving the horse some strokes, Logan handed her the reins. "Why don't you do a couple of laps with him? He needs the exercise. Today has been the first time I've taken him out of the stall since he arrived here. And it took three carrots."

She laughed. "Come on, Domino. We both could use the exercise." She tugged on his lead rope and they began to walk.

Logan leaned back against the fence and followed their movements. He told himself he was watching for any limping from the horse, but it was hard not to watch Tori as well. She was open and loving, building a strong bond with Domino. The gelding was starting to trust her.

Winning Tori's trust wouldn't be easy. Something in her past had her nearly as skittish as Domino, especially men. He hadn't missed the fact that every time he'd gotten close, he felt her body tense.

That was probably a good thing. He didn't need to get involved with her, not short term or long term. Tori Slater didn't seem like the type who had brief affairs with a man. He suspected a relationship was all or nothing for her.

That didn't mean he didn't want to taste her mouth, to feel her sweet curves pressed up against him. He caught the gentle sway of her hips, her tiny waist that would fit in the span of his hands. She was a beautiful woman. Her dark eyes made him think of hot sultry nights making love. He cursed, feeling his body stir to life.

"Logan?"

He came back to the present. "What?"

"Do you want me to keep walking Domino?"

Logan shook his head. "Nah, I think he's had enough. Domino can go back into his stall. He feels more secure there."

Logan took the reins from her and they led the horse into the cool barn. Once in the stall, he wiped down the animal with a cloth, but didn't use a brush, knowing he got jumpy when touched in the hindquarters. Tori kept talking to the gelding, keeping him calm.

Once finished with the grooming, Logan walked out and latched the gate. "Are you ready to see the bunkhouse?"

Tori nodded, but still had her gaze on the horse. "Will Domino ever be able to trust?"

Logan shrugged. "Not sure. It's very doubtful he'll make a good saddle horse. Time will tell."

Tori climbed on the bottom rung of the railing and reached out a hand and the horse came to her. "It's okay, boy. We won't hurt you ever." She pressed her face to his, stroking his muzzle. "You're safe now." Tears pooled in her eyes when she finally backed away. "See you later, Domino."

Logan was silent as they walked out the back door. No matter how hard he tried, he couldn't stop being aware of this woman. Not just her presence, but her soft scent that seemed to fill his senses with every breath he took. He had to figure out how to deal with her being around. She wasn't easy to resist, but he had to keep this all about business.

They made their way to the long dormitory-like building. "The outside looks nice," Tori said.

Logan looked at the glossy white structure. "My grandfather liked to keep up things."

Tori smiled. "I'm glad he did."

Inside, there was a large mud room with a washer and dryer and a deep sink at the far end. "The anglers can use this area for their equipment. There's also room for a freezer to store their catch. Right outside there's a water source to clean and gut the fish. I suggest adding a stainless steel counter to keep it sanitary."

Tori looked at Logan with wide eyes. "You've thought of a lot things I never would have. I take it you're a fisherman."

He shrugged. "On occasion I've been known to drop a line in the water. Hard not to with the river and streams around here."

"I hope there's a lot of other people who think the same."

He followed her through another doorway and into a large community room with two old sofas, two recliners and a small television. The floors were tiled, and they didn't seem to be in bad shape.

She went over to the kitchen area and began opening the cabinets to find dishes, pots and pans.

"With some cleaning and a little paint, it's not bad."

"I hadn't been inside this place in a while," he said as they continued down a hall that led to four bedrooms.

The rooms weren't that large, but big enough for a double bed and dresser. Two large bathrooms were also situated between the rooms. Then at the end of the hall was a dorm-style room with five single beds.

She looked at him and titled her head. "What do you think? With some new mattresses could we rent this out?"

He shrugged. "I don't see a problem. You've got three private rooms. Most men would rather be here instead of sleeping in their truck or boat or in a tent on the ground. Clara could give you a better idea of what anglers want and what to charge. Maybe toss in coffee and a basic breakfast."

She nodded. "Now, could you take me to see some of these perfect fishing spots? I don't want to advertise something I can't deliver."

"Sure." He needed to put some distance between them. But first he had to finish the work on the cabin, the bunkhouse and show her the best fishing. Then he could get on with his plans. Why didn't that sound more appealing?

***

Two days later, Tori rose early to be ready for her busy day. After Logan had showed her the fishing spots, she didn't have any doubts she could open the private area for fishing.

She had her family on board with the project and they promised to send her money to help prepare the bunkhouse. She needed to talk with Clara to see if she could get any business.

She was planning to make the trip into Dawson Springs on her own and give Logan a break from her. She couldn't keep depending on this man and taking up all of his time. Plus they'd spent a lot of time together, and she discovered she liked his company, too much. She needed to be more independent, especially since she was going to run this business herself.

Her first job was to drive into town, but when she opened the cabin door she found Logan leaning against his truck as sexy as could be. A definite poster boy for the perfect cowboy, except Logan McNeely wasn't a boy.

He explained he needed more wood to finish the railing and he offered to drive her. So much for ignoring the man.

Twenty minutes later, they pulled up in front of the general store. Tori said, "You can just drop me off and I'll talk to Clara while you get the wood."

"Not a problem." Logan got out of the truck.

Tori gave up and climbed out, too. She walked toward the general store where he held open the door, waiting. She stepped inside and heard a bell sound.

"I'll be with you in a second," a familiar voice called out from the back.

Tori walked around and eventually found the sporting goods section. She examined the row of rods and reels. Some had pretty hefty price tags. "I guess I missed this department the other day."

Logan came up beside her. "There's so much in the store, that's easy to do. The good thing is Clara carries pretty much about anything you'll ever need."

"That's nice to know, because I'll need to buy some towels and sheets just for starters." The family provided her a budget to help get things off and running. She was surprised her sisters hadn't decided to descend upon her. That made her both happy and nervous. Making this venture a success was her responsibility.

The middle-aged woman came out of a back room. "Sorry to keep you waiting, but I got a phone call," Clara said as she walked in.

She smiled. "Well, hello you two." She went and hugged Tori. "I was wondering how you were getting along out there."

"I'm doing all right," Tori admitted. "Logan's been replacing the cabin's rotted porch, and I've been making some decisions about the ranch. I'm hoping you can help me."

Clara's eyes widened. "Sure. What do you need?"

Tori smiled. "I hear you're an expert about the fishing in this area. My family has decided to open Colton Creek to anglers. My first question to you is would I get any business?"

Tori went on to tell Clara about her plans to put up the guests in the bunkhouse.

Clara smiled. "My goodness, I'd say you've been busy this past week."

Tori stole a quick glance at Logan, knowing he'd helped her a lot. "We need to make the ranch financially solvent. And since Colt hasn't paid much attention to the homestead in a few years, we need to change that. Fishing seems to be one of the best ways to bring in quick money."

Clara nodded. "In the next few weeks this area will be swarming with anglers. I'd say your chances are pretty good. If you want, you can put up an advertisement here in the store. And I also have an outfitter, Josh Snyder, who works through the store. I could send him to the ranch to have a look at what you have to offer. How soon will you be ready for guests?"

Excitement churned inside Tori. "That sounds good, but I'll need at least another week.
And I'll also need someone who wants to help out with cleaning and some painting at the ranch."

Clare gave her the name and number of a handy man. "So Colt's fine with opening up his ranch?"

Tori remembered what Logan told her about a relationship between the two. "My father has changed his views on a lot of things lately. Besides, he doesn't have a choice. This ranch needs to bring in some money."

"I'd hate to see you lose your family's homestead. The Coltons were one of the original settlers in this area."

Glad to find someone who valued history, Tori nodded. "And it's important to us that we keep the place for future generations."

"Well, then let's see if we can drum up some business," Clara told her and looked at Logan. "This guy here has been out there by himself too long."

"Clara, I'm fine with my own company."

So there wasn't a woman in Logan's life. Not that it was any of her business. "Thanks for your help, Clara. I'll get back to you when I have a sign for your store." She made a mental note to have her sister put together a few flyers and send them. Of course, she would put together a website herself. Tori started for the door with Logan close behind.

"Wait, I almost forgot," Clara called to them as she hurried to the front of the store. "If you want to meet a lot of the townspeople, there's the Dawson Springs Annual Social this Saturday and Sunday."

"I've seen a sign or two around town," Tori said. "Guess I've been too busy to even ask about it."

"Well, most everyone in town and the surrounding area attends. We have a farmer's market and craft fair during the day. The event turns into a barbecue that helps support the school, and then there's a dance to top off the night."

"Sounds like quite an event."

Clara nodded. "The biggest Dawson Springs has all year. It really helps promote the local business and economy. And you'll get to know your neighbors." She reached behind the cash register and grabbed a stack of tickets. "I can guarantee you'll have fun."

Tori wasn't sure she was interested in coming into town by herself, or being the center of attention. "Well, maybe I can buy a ticket and I'll have to see if I can make it."

She reached for her purse to for some money. "I'll donate for two tickets, Clara."

The older woman beamed. "What would really be nice if you both came and enjoyed yourselves. Life can't be all about work."

***

Later Tori went to the lumberyard with Logan and walked straight to the paint department. She decided not to stray too far from the color already on the walls so maybe one coat would do.

She tried to stay excited about her project, but all she could think about was the town social. Was Clara playing matchmaker? Did Logan feel obligated to buy the ticket? She hated situations like this. She'd never been good playing the dating game. Not that this was anything like a date. She never dated men like Logan, the big physical types. At least those types had never noticed her.

"Did your find a color?"

Tori turned to see Logan. "Who knew there were so many choices for white?" She held up a color card. "They're mixing five gallons of this one. And I got brushes, rollers and some drop clothes. I think it's everything I need."

He nodded. "I've loaded the wood in the truck. You need anything else?"

"I know we're running late, but would you mind if I stop by the market? I'm about out of food."

He shook his head. "No, you go on ahead. I'll load everything in the truck and meet you at the coffee shop. Might as well stay for lunch."

She nodded. "Okay, but this time it's my treat." With determined steps, she quickly walked off before he could argue.

Logan watched the gentle sway of her hips, but he wasn't the only one. The new woman in town was getting a lot of male interest.

"Hey, McNeely."

Logan turned to see the sheriff, Tom Harris. The big, burly man was about fifty with thick gray hair and a ready smile, but you still wouldn't want to cross the retired marine. "Hey, Sheriff. How is it going?"

"Not bad. I hear we have a new resident." He smiled at Tori across the room. "She's a pretty little thing. I can see why you've been hiding her out at the ranch."

Logan tried not to overreact. "I'm not hiding anyone. Tori's family owns the Colton Creek. She's been busy with repairs on the place."

"I take it you're helping her?"

"Since the Slaters pay me, yes, I'm helping her repair the porch."

The man's grin didn't stop. "Nice to know someone is out there with her. That place is pretty isolated."

Logan refused to be pulled into any small town gossip. "I need to get back to work." He said his goodbyes to everyone, then walked out and put the paint in the bed of the truck beside the wood and nails.

Next stop was the post office. He walked into the small annex and saw the one employee, Molly Hawkins. "Hey, Molly, you got anything for me today?"

The sixty-year-old didn't smile. "Just the same thing we all get bills and junk mail."

He took the stack and started to leave.

"Wait a minute," she called. "Here's the mail for Miss Tori Slater. It's one of those express envelopes. Some people can't wait to get things these days."

"Thanks Molly, I'll give it to her."

The gray-haired woman nodded. "I don't doubt you will since I saw you drive her into town." She studied him. "Extend an invitation to her to come to the Dawson Springs Community Church this Sunday. The service starts at ten o'clock. Wouldn't hurt you to show up, too."

"I'll pass on the invite." He turned and walked out before she could pry anymore. He made another stop at the drug store and picked up a couple personal items, not wanting to end up at the market with Tori. Just what the town's residents needed was more ammo for the gossip mill. Right now, he wished he could rethink the idea of him bringing her into town.

After paying for his purchase, he walked across the street to the Good Morning Café. He went inside to find the place busy. *Great.* He usually sat at the counter, but today a booth might be better. He sat and looked around the fifties style diner with the worn linoleum black and white floor and the red vinyl booths. There were print curtains in the windows.

The waitress, Caroline, brought him a glass of water and the coffeepot.

Without saying a word, Logan turned over his cup on the table and she filled it. She usually flirted with him, but he refused to give her any encouragement. For one thing she was too young for him, and another, he wasn't interested.

She gave him a forced smile. "What can I get you, Logan?"

"Just coffee for now, Caroline. I'm waiting for someone. Could you bring another water?"

"Sure." She walked off just as the door opened.

Tori stepped inside. Suddenly, she became the center of attention as everyone turned in her direction. A slight blush crossed her face.

In reaction, his protective instincts kicked in. He stood and went to her.

When she spotted him, she smiled, a gesture that warmed her eyes. He felt that jolt in his gut again.

"Good, you're already here," she said sounding a little breathless.

"I just arrived." He placed his hand against her lower back and directed her to their booth.

She put her purse on the seat beside her. "I put the groceries in the backseat of the truck. Thank you for leaving it unlocked."

"That's what's nice about a small town; it's pretty safe." He smiled. "And they don't want to have to deal with the sheriff." To keep from staring, he opened the menu. He wanted to eat and get out of here. "He's a nice guy, if you don't cross him."

She smiled as she picked up the menu. "Sounds like you've had some personal experience."

His jaw tensed. "Our paths have crossed a few times over the years."

Just then the waitress reappeared and set down a second glass of water. "My, my, Logan." She turned her attention to Tori. "You've been holding out on us."

***

"You ready to go?" Logan asked.

Tori took the last bite of her sandwich and swallowed hard, but managed a nod. This lunch was the fastest she'd even eaten. Not that she minded leaving the café, not with everyone watching her. And it seemed that Caroline couldn't take her gaze off Logan. Had Logan dated the waitress?

They climbed into the truck. "Is Caroline a friend of yours?" she asked as she fastened her seatbelt.

He glanced across to her, his eyes intense. The look caused her stomach to tighten in awareness. He backed up and drove through town. "No, I've avoided her mostly."

Why did that make her happy? "She's pretty."

"I don't date much. I haven't managed to find the time."

"I guess you've been busy."

The rest of the drive to the ranch was quiet, but from experience she knew Logan liked it that way. He wasn't a talker. He pulled off the highway onto the gravel road that led away from the Colton Creek.

"Is this a shortcut?" she asked as she gazed around.

He shook his head. "I need to pick up some power tools at my place. We're only a couple of miles apart, even closer on horseback."

Tori felt some comfort in knowing Logan would still be close, even when he moved back to his ranch. She either had to hire someone else, or do things on her own.

"You know, if you need room to work the horses, you can continue to use our corral." Brows furrowed, he glanced sideways.

She rushed on. "I mean you've done so much to help me. Besides the barn and corral aren't being used now."

"Thanks for the offer," he said. I'll think about it. Domino might be better off for now at your place."

Oh, Domino. She would miss him.

The road grew bumpy as Logan rode them under an archway that read, Double M Ranch, then he continued along the gravel road as a two-story house came into view.

Logan felt uncomfortable with Tori's scrutiny as she looked around. The house looked like hell with the paint peeling off the shiplap. For the past few years, he'd put all his energy and time into building a new corral and repairing the outer buildings.

The barn was a lot smaller than the one at the homestead, but the structure was efficient enough with fresh paint and new stalls. Getting enthusiastic was hard since his grandfather wasn't around to share the dream.

"Nate used your larger corral to break the mustangs," he told her. "When he got sick and was in bed for several weeks before he died, he could watch the mustangs from the window in the apartment."

"I'm sorry. I would have loved to meet him."

Swallowing hard, Logan nodded, surprised how much he still felt the loss.

He got out of the truck, unlocked the garage and lifted the door. Inside was his workshop. When he was recovering from his injury, he came out here, played around with his grandfather's tools and began building things.

"Oh, Logan, this is beautiful."

He looked over his shoulder, surprised to find Tori had followed him into the garage. She was staring at a piece of furniture he'd built a long time ago. A simple cabinet with upper and lower flat-front doors divided by a counter and a long drawer in the middle. He'd seen it in a catalog. "It's called a Hoosier cabinet."

"I know. There's one similar to this in our kitchen at the Lazy S." Her dark eyes were bright with wonder. "You built this?"

He nodded. "A long time ago."

Her lips curved into a smile. "Seems I have an expert carpenter fixing the porch."

"It's a hobby." He pulled tools out of the cabinets. He placed them in the bed of the truck, then wheeled out a long cylindrical looking machine. "It's an air compressor," he told her. "It will help power the nail gun. The porch railing will go much faster."

Tori caught one of his rare smiles, and it made her feel light-hearted. It had been a long time since she felt at ease with a man. Would it be possible to leave all the bad stuff behind and move on?

When he walked back into the garage, she asked, "Is there anything I can do to help?"

"There's a box of nail strips in the cabinet over the washing machine inside the house."

Tori climbed the single step that led to a utility room with an old washer and dryer. Above them, she found the box of nails, but instead of returning to the garage, her curiosity got to her and she peered through another doorway and found the kitchen. The area was small and although clean, the cabinets were old and the linoleum worn. There was a hutch with several photos perched on the shelf.

Drawn inside, she went to have a look. The first one was of a younger looking Logan and beside him stood an older man with thinning white hair she assumed was his grandfather. Nate McNeely had been as tall as his grandson and they had the same smile. Eager to see more, she spotted a group of photos on a table. She went to them and pick up another where Logan was a teenager dressed in a baseball uniform. She smiled, seeing he was a serious kid even then. She went to the next one and paused, seeing the man she'd met just a week ago, looking back at her in a uniform.

Logan McNeely was a Denver Police Officer? She couldn't be more surprised. Was he still working for them? Would he go back?

She heard Logan come into the room and she turned, the picture still in her grasp. "Are you really a rancher, or a police officer?"

"I'm a rancher now."

"You just walked away from your career?"

"Yes, I did."

She opened her mouth to ask more.

"Some of us don't talk about our past. Maybe because it's not anyone's business," Logan told her. "Kind of like that letter you received the other day."

Tori's face heated and she put down the picture. "I apologize, Logan. I had no business snooping around. I was just caught by surprise."

"I spent seven years on the Denver Police Force." He hesitated. "I was wounded and didn't go back. Instead, I came here. End of story." He grabbed the bag of nails off the table and walked out. She had no choice, but to follow him.

CHAPTER SIX

The next morning, Tori got up early and quickly got busy at work on a website design for the new venture.

Fishing on Colton Creek Ranch. Trout aplenty, Brown, Rainbow and Golden. Bunkhouse-style lodging, breakfast included. Private rooms available. Colton Family proprietors.

Concentrating on her job had been hard with the rhythmic sound of the nail gun and the occasional noise from the air compressor.

Her thoughts went back to yesterday and the trip back from the Double M Ranch. Neither she nor Logan spoke of the pictures again. That didn't mean she'd put the fact out of her mind. How do you go from a Denver police officer to living on a ranch in Wyoming?

His change sounded ridiculously close to what she was doing. What was he escaping from? Could it be he got tired of that lifestyle? Of course, he got shot. That would be enough to leave. Whatever the reason, he hadn't wanted to talk about it, and she had to respect his privacy. Too bad she couldn't stop wondering that there might be something else he didn't tell.

She sighed. "Looks like we both have secrets, Mr. McNeely."

She clicked on her email and found a note from her sister, telling her she'd sent a copy of Dane's letter to Detective Brandon.

Tori closed her eyes. Why couldn't Dane just move on, leave her alone?

"Tori?" a familiar voice called.

She opened her eyes and found Logan standing just inside the open door of the cabin.

"Oh, I didn't hear you come in. I was lost in my thoughts, coming up with some ideas for the webpage." She stood and went toward him.

There were beads of perspiration on his face and neck. He removed his hat and wiped his shirt sleeve across his face. "Damn, it's getting hot out there."

Good Lord, the man was handsome in his T-shirt, low slung jeans and tool belt. She forced her attention back to his face, but had to glance away. It wasn't supposed to be this way. She wasn't supposed to feel that shimmer of desire, the yearning. The sudden awareness shocked her.

"I'm sorry. Of course, you can't work in this heat."

He arched an eyebrow. "I'm nearly finished anyway, but I need to get over to the bunkhouse."

He was distracting her. "The bunkhouse?"

"Yeah, the two men we hired to clear out the place and do the painting started this morning. I thought I'd stop by and see how they're doing. I'll come back here later to finish the porch when the sun goes behind the cabin."

She nodded. "Of course, take your time."

Careful to avoid touching, she stepped around him and went outside to the covered porch to find the new floor completed. He'd framed the top railing and was adding the pickets. On the front, he'd attached lattice to keep animals from getting under the floor. She'd already thought about planting some flowers along the front side. Satisfied with the progress, she came back inside.

Logan had used tap water to wash his face and now was drinking deeply from a glass.

"You've gotten so much done already."

He nodded. "That's why I started early."

She'd heard him at dawn. "You don't have to ask me for permission to stop."

He smiled. "Thanks, boss." He started to walk off but stopped and turned. "Why don't you come with me and see for yourself what's going on?"

"Sure, if you need me."

"I'm not the boss, you are."

Jamming her hands into her back pockets, she smiled. "I guess I am. Will you be working in the bunkhouse, too?"

"If I'm needed, but these guys are working pretty cheap. So I thought I'd take off a few hours." With a glint in his eye, he studied her a moment. "You want to play hooky with me?"

She felt a surge of excitement, but couldn't help but be leery. "I really should work on the website to get it ready to go live."

He shrugged. "I'll have to go riding by myself."

"Riding?" Excitement crept into her tone.

His Stetson shaded his face. "I'm checking on the mustang herd. A couple of the mares are pregnant." He came closer. "What do you say? We can take the trail along the river where it's shaded and cooler. So, you want to go?"

She couldn't hide her enthusiasm. He wanted her to come along? "Yes, I want to go. Can I ride Buffy again?"

He nodded. "But this time, you're gonna saddle her."

"Not a problem." With a few deft clicks, she shut down her laptop. "Let me grab my camera so I can get some pictures for the website. I'll meet you at the bunkhouse.

"Good idea."

She hurried upstairs, grabbed her camera, and came back downstairs to get her phone. She decided to make a couple of sandwiches, added two apples, and bottled water then slipped them in a small knapsack.

She walked across the compound to the bunkhouse as the sound of music came from inside. Old mattresses were tossed on the ground outside along with ladders and drop clothes.

When she went through the door, she found more furniture pushed to the middle of the big room, and the two men, Harry and Juan, in white painter's uniforms taping off the windows.

Logan walked in her direction, and waved for the men. The radio was turned off and both guys came close.

"Tori, you remember, Juan and Harry?"

"Yes, I do. Looks like you've been working hard this morning."

The middle-aged Harry spoke up. "Yes, ma'am. You said a week, and we'll have it done well before then."

"Good. If you need anything, I'm usually at the cabin."

Logan stepped in. "You also have my cell phone number." He put his hand against Tori's back. "We'll be gone for a few hours to check the herd."

She said her goodbyes, then walked out with slow steps. "Maybe we should stay and help."

He gave her a sideways glance. "We're paying them to do the work. Besides, they need this job. And if we stay, we can't go riding."

"Well, I wouldn't want to spoil your plans." With a laugh, she picked up her pace to catch up with him.

Once in the barn, she stopped by Domino's stall. The horse came to the gate and greeted her. "Hey, guy." She rubbed the animal's forehead. "So how is everything today?"

The horse blew out a breath and nodded his head. She smiled. "Maybe I'll come back later and we'll take a walk."

She hurried down the aisle as Logan came out of the tack room carrying a saddle. He directed her to the tack he'd laid out for her. Logan was a good man to have around. That thought surprised her since she wasn't sure she'd ever be able to trust a man again.

***

Logan wondered why he'd asked Tori to come along. He'd planned to get away for a few hours from all the distractions. He usually rode because he liked being alone. His grandfather had understood when he had to get away.

Riding along the split-rail fence, Logan looked out at the cattle that dotted the incredible vistas. The sound of the rushing stream and the cooling breeze gave him the contentment he strived for. The sight made him wonder how he could have ever left here.

Since the shooting two years ago, he'd carried the blame for the screw up, for trusting the wrong person. In the process, he'd let so many people down.

He felt Tori approach as the trail widened. He slowed Ace to a walk so they could ride side by side. She'd been his biggest distraction since her arrival just a little over a week ago. Somehow, he let her intrude in his solitary life. If that hadn't been enough, the petite woman with sexy bedroom eyes and a full mouth that begged to be kissed had invaded his dreams, too. He'd had an endless list of fantasies with her as the star. He shook his head. Tori Slater was only here temporarily, and that was the way he liked it.

"How are you doing?"

"Great." She had the camera strap around her neck, waiting for the next photo op. "I got some wonderful shots along the creek. Sorry if I'm holding you up. Once I learn my way around the ranch, I can go off on my own." She patted the horse. "Of course, I'll need my own mount once you move Buffy back to your place."

"There's no hurry. I'll be around for awhile." He didn't want to think about her out here on her own. "But you probably should hire someone to live on the property."

"Maybe if I get enough business, I can hire a married couple and they can live in the apartment over the bunkhouse." She rushed on to say. "That is whenever you need to get back to your ranch."

She waved her hand. "I don't want to talk about business today. It's too beautiful out here." A breeze kicked up, and the air was cooling off. "Are you hungry? It's not much, but I brought some sandwiches."

He adjusted his hat. "Sounds good. How about we eat under those trees?" They picked up the pace and made it the shade of a group of old oaks.

Once they dismounted and watered the horses, Logan took a small bedroll off his saddle and spread it in front of a fallen tree trunk.

He glanced out toward the water. "Thanks to the reservoir, this creek is nearly overflowing most of the year. Good fishing, too."

"I'm counting on that." Tori brought her bag to the blanket and sat. She pulled out three sandwiches and put two in front of him. "It's just ham with mustard and there's an apple."

"Thanks." He sat and leaned against the log, then took a bite. "Tastes good."

Tori wondered why she didn't feel uncomfortable being alone with Logan. Probably because he'd been around her so much the past week. It was a good thing, since she was trying to form a partnership with the man.

"I talked to my sisters last night about the idea of raising organic beef."

Logan turned to her as he swallowed. "You're not wasting any time."

She shook her head. "I've been doing some research online. It seems to be a good direction to go. My sisters agree. They're presenting the idea to Colt." She took a bite of her sandwich, then added, "My father might be a harder sell."

"I've noticed you call him either, your father, or Colt."

She shrugged, trying to act like it didn't bother her. "We weren't really close while I was growing up. When our mother left, Colt didn't handle it well. He more or less forgot he had four daughters to raise."

"I'm sorry. I only met the man a few times, but he seemed really proud of his girls."

"Wish we could have seen that side of him."

They continued to eat in silence, then Tori said, "It was Nate who raised you."

Taking off his hat, Logan scooted down and leaned back against the log. His grandfather seemed to be a safe topic. "He was the best. Better than I deserved most of the time."

"How long did you live with him?"

"I was ten when my parents died in a small plane crash. When I first arrived, I gave him a bushel of trouble. Some involved local law enforcement."

She smiled. "I take it, you were a handful?"

"I had a big chip on my shoulder and was daring anyone to try and knock it off. I was angry my parents were dead, and I was stuck out here in the middle of nowhere. Nate was pretty tolerant." He stole a glance to see she was listening intently. "That's probably why he was so patient with the mustangs. I gave him plenty of practice."

"You seem to have turned out pretty well."

His gaze locked on hers. "I wish I could take back those bad years I wasted so much time, time I could have spent with a pretty great guy."

She blinked back tears. "I bet your grandfather knew how much you loved him. You took care of him when he got sick."

"But he took care of me so many more times."

She reached over and covered his hand. "That's because he loved you, too, Logan."

Getting lost in those dark eyes of hers was so easy. "Why does it take so long to realize how good you have things before it's all taken away?"

"Because we're human, Logan, and because we make mistakes in life."

He felt himself drift toward her as her head lowered to his. "I've made a hell of a lot of them."

"So have I. I believed..."

She stopped and tried to pull away.

But he reached out, cupped her cheek and made her look at him.

"What, Tori?"

"I was naïve about relationships." Her inky-black lashes lowered over those incredible eyes. "I trusted someone I shouldn't have."

"Good to be a little guarded. I'll always tell you the truth, Tori." He hesitated. "And right now, I want to kiss you more than I want my next breath." She didn't resist when he drew her to him and covered her mouth with his.

Oh, God. This was far beyond any dream he could ever have. He kept his passion under control but just barely. His mouth gentled on hers, but it stirred a longing he'd never experienced before.

When she whimpered softly and leaned closer, he teased her lips and when they parted, slipped his tongue inside to taste her. She reacted too, pressing her breasts to his chest. God help him.

He reluctantly broke off the kiss, but not the contact as his mouth trailed along her jawline until he reached her ear, and he breathed, "I've wanted to do that from the second I saw you."

She raised her gaze to meet his.

In an instant, he saw her wariness.

"Logan... this is a bad idea."

He heard the tears in her voice. His chest tightened, but he didn't want her to pull away, but he knew he couldn't push her. He released her and sat up, too. "It's okay, Tori. I don't know who you're used to, but I'd never push you into something you don't want."

As she sat upright and stared out toward the mountains she gazed for several moments in silence. "It's not you, Logan. I'm not good at this."

The hell she wasn't. He got the feeling her fear was connected to the letter she'd gotten the other day. "That's the problem, you're very good at this."

She finally turned around, but didn't make eye contact. "Please, can we just go find the mustangs?"

"Sure, as long as you're okay." Somehow he was relieved she still wanted to have him around. But it would be better if she kicked him to the curb. At least, safer for both of them.

***

"See, look over there," Logan whispered as he pointed. "In the sage brush."

Kneeling on the ground, partly hidden by a group of blue spruce, Tori couldn't help but be aware of Logan beside her as she aimed the camera with the long-range lens. She could feel his heat, his strength. She had trouble concentrating on the herd of mustangs grazing in the pasture.

"How many are there?"

"I've counted as many as eighteen," he said as he used binoculars. "Now add in two new foals."

"They're so cute." Tori zoomed in on the new deliveries, trying for a good camera shot. She took several. "My sister Marissa is the photographer in the family. She could do a lot better job."

Suddenly, she heard a loud whinny and looked toward the west to see a large sorrel stallion approaching the herd. He tossed his head as he flung his flaxen mane in a mating dance, drawing attention. And he got it, but from another stallion in the herd.

More high-pitched whinnies filled the air as the two males reared up on their hind legs and soon the fight for dominance began.

Tori quickly became aware of the animals' sexual prowess. "Oh, my," she breathed. "They're magnificent."

"We named the sorrel, Chief. This is his herd of mares. But that young chestnut stallion, Red Rider, wants to take over as the dominant stallion of the herd."

Tori had heard stories about the mustangs, now she was experiencing it firsthand. "Can't they just share?" she asked, watching the fighting equines.

Logan leaned into her space. He was so close she could feel his breath against her face. "Males don't share."

She couldn't look away, recalling the kiss they'd shared just moments ago. She felt tightening low in her stomach. He started to move toward her when she heard another loud whinny, and she turned back to the horses. Just in time to see the sorrel stallion mount a shiny black mare eager to reward the victor. She had to bite back a moan, seeing the raw, fervent mating.

"It's survival of the fittest in the wild," he said in a low husky voice. "Are you strong enough to handle all this?"

***

The ride back to the ranch had been quiet and Logan hadn't felt the need to make conversation. He'd already made too many mistakes. His first mistake had been even suggesting she go riding with him. When he should have been leaving her alone, he ended up kissing her.

When they arrived back at the barn, he convinced her to let him handle the horses. She reluctantly agreed and walked off to the cabin, leaving him in peace. Although he didn't feel very peaceful, not when she had stirred up things pretty good.

He released the cinch strap on Buffy and pulled the saddle off her back, then carried it to the tack room. He repeated the same scenario on

Ace until the chore was done. He'd planned to continue work on the porch, but he didn't need to be around Tori anymore today. Safer for the both of them if he kept his distance.

So he headed to the bunkhouse to check on the painters' progress. He was surprised to see most of the main room was done and Juan promised to come back early and finish the job tomorrow.

Logan gave them a key and headed off to the apartment upstairs. He glanced around the area. The place wasn't that small, but the space suddenly seemed so sterile, so lonely. Wasn't that the way he wanted it? Didn't he want to be left alone?

He marched across the living space to the first of two bedrooms, the one he'd slept in the past six months. With a quick jerk, he pulled off his boots, then removed his shirt and jeans. In the small bathroom, he turned on the shower, then stripped out of his briefs and climbed in under the spray. The hot water eased the stress and sore muscles of the day, then his thoughts turned to Tori as he began to wash. How it felt with her body pressed against him, that sweet mouth of hers hungry for him. He groaned and turned the water to cold and quickly finished the shower. Once out, he dried off, wrapped the towel around his waist, and began to shave. Once the job was completed, he put away the razor, then he heard a knock on the door.

Who? Probably the painters. He went to the door and pulled it open to find Tori. Those dark eyes widened when she saw him.

"Oh, I'm sorry, Logan. This isn't a good time." Gaze averted, she started off the step.

"Tori wait. Must be important or you wouldn't come by."

She couldn't meet his eyes. "It's probably nothing."

He tensed. "What's probably nothing?"

She released a long breath and lifted her head. "I think someone has been in the cabin."

***

With Logan's insistence, Tori came inside the apartment while he stepped down the hallway to get dressed. She closed her eyes and pictured the man standing in the open doorway in just a towel. She groaned, recalling the broad shoulders and muscular chest and arms. She couldn't stop her gaze as she took in the six-pack stomach, and she didn't miss what had marred that perfection. A large scar ran along his side, just below his ribcage. He'd told her he'd been shot, but seeing the wound...

He walked back into the room, dressed in fresh jeans and shirt, and carrying his boots. He sat down on the sofa and pulled on his socks.

"You said someone has been inside the cabin. Was anything taken?"

She shook her head, concentrating on what happened. "I'm probably just imagining this, but several things were out of place."

Her heart began to race as he stood and buttoned his shirt. "Well, let's go and have a second look."

Grabbing his jacket, Logan opened the door, scanned the immediate area and let her go ahead of him down the steep steps. The late afternoon was a little chilly and a breeze picked up as they headed across the compound. The temperature was doing nothing to cool him off. Today, he'd gotten too close to Tori, and finding her on his doorstep with a definite interested look in her eyes hadn't helped. If he hadn't planned to keep his distance, he could come up with a completely different scenario.

"Have you ever had trouble with break-ins?" she asked.

He shook his head. "Maybe a raccoon or curious bear, but not of the human kind, but I'm not dismissing your claim." That was why he had his Glock tucked in the back of his jeans. Just in case.

They made their way up the new steps and Logan eyed the half completed railing. "I'll get this finished tomorrow."

"I'm not worried about it right now."

He paused on the porch to see his stack of lumber had been scattered around along with the box of nails. Someone or something had been here. He paused at the door and wondered how to handle this.

"Stay behind me."

She shrugged. "There's no one here. I'm feeling silly about asking you to come by."

The last thing he thought about Tori was silly. She was articulate and well organized. With deliberate moves, he opened the door and went inside. His expert eyes searched for anyone around the main room.

He checked the rooms downstairs then climbed the steps to continue his search on the second floor. He peered inside Tori's bedroom and caught a whiff of her scent. It distracted him momentarily, but he headed for the closet and looked inside. Her clothes were neatly hung along the railing. He shut the armoire and turned to find her standing nearby.

"Okay, you can tell me I'm crazy."

"I'm not gonna do that. Tell me what was different."

She went to the dresser where a silver locket laid on the top. "I didn't put that there. It was in my jewelry box in the drawer."

"What else?" he asked.

She pulled open the middle dresser drawer. It was filled with lingerie, all soft pastel colors and silky fabrics.

He swallowed, fighting the immediate picture of her he'd conjured up in his head. "Is there something missing?"

"No, but I fold all my things." She waved a hand at the jumbled mess. "I've never put anything away like this, just ask my twin sister, Josie."

Okay, that got his attention. “Show me more.”

“The bed, too. The sheets are messed up under the blanket.”

She took him downstairs into the bathroom to show him more disorder in her makeup drawer. They moved onto the old trunk where she kept her great-great-grandmother’s things.

She lifted the lid of the cedar chest, exposing another mess inside. “Looks like someone was looking for something, maybe money.”

“If so, don’t you think they’d take your computer and jewelry?”

As he glanced around the room, he ran over the items involved. He had a hunch this was more personal. “Do you know why anyone would come inside and not take anything?” He paused. “And just want to let you know he’s been here.”

Her eyes widened, but she didn’t say anything.

“Maybe it’s time you tell me about the guy who sent you that letter

CHAPTER SEVEN

"You want my help, Tori, then you better start sharing some information," Logan told her. "If it's your ex-boyfriend and you've just had a lover's quarrel, I don't want any part of it." He started for the door wondering why the hell he was angry about that.

"Dane's an ex-boyfriend, but it's been eight months since we've been together."

Logan turned around. "Maybe he hasn't gotten the message."

She looked at him, but her eyes wouldn't meet his. "I don't know how he found me here."

"So that letter was from him?"

She nodded slowly. "He was smart enough not to sign it, but I know it was from him."

"Let me see it," he demanded, not caring if she heard the anger in his voice.

She hesitated then went to her computer and pulled up a file.

Logan followed her and read the note. It didn't take long for him to see that the guy had mental problems.

Vicki,

Although I miss you, I'm glad you're home with your family. This will give you time to think about us and remember how good it was. Even if people try to keep us apart, you know we belong together. Sooner or later you'll realize it, too.

Always, D

"Why is this on your computer? What happened to the original letter?"

"I sent it to Detective Brandon in Los Angeles."

Police are involved? Logan didn't like where this was going. "So I take it this, D..." he paused.

"Dane Buckley," she filled in.

"This Buckley guy has bothered you before."

She nodded. "Not up until this note and now."

He could tell she wasn't telling him everything. "Look, I know you want to forget all this, but if he is hanging around, he could be a loose cannon." He knew this type too well. "Is there any way Buckley could have discovered you came here? Did you ever mention this ranch when you were together?"

As she paced, she shook her head. "No, I didn't know about Colton Creek until I moved away from LA. I haven't talked to Dane since our breakup. Everything has been handled through Detective Brandon."

Logan frowned. "A police detective?"

She nodded. "I got a restraining order against Dane because he wouldn't leave me alone."

Logan cursed under his breath. This explained so much, her fear of him getting too close. "This guy has been stalking you?"

"Three months ago, he trashed Josie's townhouse where I lived." She sighed and her shoulders slumped. "It had been so long since Dane had done anything, I thought I was safe." Her eyes filled with tears and her arms wrapped around her waist. "How did he find me here?"

"We still don't know that he has, but you need to let Sheriff Harris know about the situation. If any stranger has been in town, maybe someone has seen him. Do you have your restraining order with you?"

She hesitated. "Do we need to do this? I mean, like you said, we don't even know if it was Dane who's been in here."

Logan had trouble remaining calm. "Do you still have feelings for this guy? Is that the reason you're protecting him?"

"No!" Her head jerked up. "The only feelings I have for Dane are disgust and anger. I don't want him in any part of my life. But yes, I have fear, too. I let him control me to the point I was ashamed of what I became." Her hands fisted. "I won't be that woman again."

"Then we'll inform the sheriff about the restraining order. And if you can come up with a picture that would be good, too."

"Okay. There's a picture on his website." She went to the keyboard and began the search.

Logan stood back and wondered how he'd let this woman get under his skin. He needed to stay detached from this whole situation. For both their sakes, he only hoped that this turned into nothing. The last thing he wanted was anyone depending on him.

Again.

***

Four days later on Saturday, Tori was headed into town for the Dawson Springs Annual Social. She'd made three pies for the event. They were apple, and they'd turned out better than she thought possible, since she was baking them in the ancient oven. Once the pies were in a box, she started out the door when Logan's truck pulled in next to her car.

She hadn't seen him much lately, not since their visit with the sheriff. Even though Tom Harris promised to keep his eye open for any strangers, Tori knew Logan had been close by, just not close enough to talk about anything too personal. That was just as well. She needed to focus on her business and getting the ranch ready.

That didn't stop her reaction when he climbed out of the truck. He was dressed in a burgundy western shirt, dark denim jeans and shiny black boots. Darn, he was one good looking cowboy.

"Hi, Logan," she said, sounding far too breathless.

"Morning, Tori. Need some help loading those?"

"I can get them, they're only apple pies," she insisted. But he'd already taken hold of the box. He carried it to his truck.

"Wait. Where are you going with those?"

He set down the box on the backseat and closed the door before she even got there. "Taking both vehicles into town seems impractical."

She felt a blush cross her cheeks. "You don't have to take me, Logan. I don't need a babysitter. I can manage to drive into town and back again on my own."

He crossed his hands over his impressive chest. "What if I want to take you?"

Suddenly, her heart rate picked up. "You mean like a date?"

He frowned. "You make it sound like it's something bad."

She smiled. "Sorry, it's just that people will think..."

"Think what? That I'm a lucky guy?"

She felt heat rise to her cheeks. "Logan, you don't have to take care of me."

Logan rested against the truck. He wasn't sure why he was doing this. He looked at Tori in her fitted jeans and that bright pink western-cut blouse and he couldn't think clearly. Only that he didn't want any other men getting a chance with her.

He leaned down and brushed his mouth across hers. At her sharp intake of breath, he raised his head. "How about I just want to spend the day with a pretty woman? And I happen to like apple pie... a lot."

He looked into her incredible eyes and then at her mouth, and suddenly his body began to heat up.

"It's my pies you want?"

If she knew what he really had on his mind, she would definitely run for the hills. "Among other things. Like maybe a dance or two later."

She finally smiled. "Okay, just let me get my purse and lock up."

He watched her turn; his gaze went to her cute backside and he groaned. He was in big trouble trying to protect her, especially since he was the one who wanted her. Bad.

***

The sunny day was perfect for a social, and Tori was enjoying herself. She'd met about half the town's population, and there was no way she could remember everyone's name.

About one in the afternoon, Clara had roped her into working the dessert booth. All the funds raised were to go to the high school athletic department. She kept busy cutting pieces of pie and cake to serve at a dollar a slice. Customers were lined up and she couldn't sell them fast enough.

"Looks like you could use some help."

Tori glanced across the table to see her neighbor. "Seth, it's good to see you."

The light-haired man smiled as he tipped his dark cowboy hat. Those whiskey colored eyes might look mischievous, but she caught the sadness in their depths. "Nice to see you again," he said and glanced around. "Where's your sidekick?"

She wasn't sure why he'd call Logan that. Did everyone think that they were involved? "If you're talking about Logan, I'm not sure. He could be spending time with the waitress from the coffee shop, Caroline."

Seth laughed. "I doubt he needs to encourage her." He studied her. "Why waste the time?"

She didn't want him to elaborate. "What can I get you?"

"How about a piece of your apple pie? I hear from the sheriff it's pretty tasty."

"So is everything on this table." She looked over yards of frosted cakes and golden pies. "Here, it's my last piece." She handed him a generous wedge on the paper plate.

"I guess this is my lucky day." He winked, dropped his dollar in the jar and walked off.

Several other men came up in her line, plus a few little kids. An odd feeling came over her, as if someone was watching her. A tingle ran down her spine. She glanced along the street. She just wished she knew for sure that Dane was far away from Wyoming.

Logan leaned against an oak tree, giving him a view of the many booths that lined Main Street. The dessert tables were his focus and the men gathered around Tori. One in particular was his friend, Seth. His busy neighbor seemed to have found time to spend with her.

"Seems Miss Slater is quite the draw."

Logan glanced over his shoulder when he recognized Tom Harris's voice. "Hello, Sheriff."

The burly man stood beside him. "Looks like you're not the only male in town who has taken an interest in our pretty new resident."

Logan ignored Harris's taunting. Even with his years in law enforcement, the sheriff couldn't forget his actions when he'd been a screwed up kid. Logan hated the fact that it still bothered him.

"Just observing." He glanced at the Sheriff. "Any news from LA about this Buckley guy?"

The older man grew serious, deepening the lines on his face. "You've worked in law enforcement, McNeely. I'd say this guy is tricky, and with his daddy having money, he was able to frighten off Tori when she started to press charges. And there's no proof he sent the letter."

"I don't doubt Buckley has been in the area," Logan told him. "His type doesn't let go easily. Not unless it's his idea."

"So we need to keep a close eye out to find him." Tom Harris grinned. "At least it gives you an excuse to stick close by her."

Keeping his gaze straight ahead, Logan refused to react and the sheriff got bored and walked off.

"Hey, cowboy."

He smiled when he saw Tori come up to him. "Hey, cowgirl."

She looked down at her jeans and western shirt and laughed. "If my friends in LA could see me now."

"Didn't they know you were raised on a ranch in Montana?"

She shook her head. "Josie and I didn't talk much about those days." She sighed. "We didn't like to think about our childhood."

Logan saw her sadness. "Your sister said Colt has changed. Maybe you can give him another chance."

She turned those big dark eyes toward him. "Sometimes, I get scared that he'll turn away again."

Logan reached out and touched her cheek. "There are no guarantees, but I know time is fleeting. And if you have the chance, take it."

She nodded.

"Come on. Let's see if we can throw away some money for a good cause." He took her hand and together they walked down the street and visited several booths.

A few hours later, Tori's arms were full of stuffed animals. "You're pretty good at this."

He picked up a baseball and aimed it at the milk cans, and then threw the perfect pitch and knocked over the cans. Tori cheered.

"We've got a winner," called the man running the booth. He leaned toward Logan and whispered, "Now, go away so we can make some money."

Logan laughed and brought Tori over. "Tori, Jack Henson, we were on the high school baseball team together."

The small man smiled. "I was more of a batboy, Logan here was the star. It's nice to meet you, Tori."

"Nice to meet you, too, Jack."

Tori watched Logan joke with his friend. She had no doubt Logan had been a popular kid. She wasn't that social while in school. In fact, she could have been called a nerd. Unlike her sister, Josie, she hadn't dated much and had never met a man like Logan McNeely.

She noticed other women watching him. Why not? He was good looking, single and babysitting her.

Logan took out his wallet and handed him a twenty. "For the sports program."

Then he came back to her wearing a big smile. "Are you having fun?"

"Yes, but honestly, Logan, you don't have to spend all your time with me."

He sobered. "Sounds like you're about to ditch me."

"Oh, no." She wanted to be with him more than she would ever admit, even to herself. "I just don't want to keep you from your friends."

He took her by the arm and headed off the main path of all the activity. He didn't stop until they were on a quiet side street. "Look, Tori, you aren't keeping me from anyone. I haven't been to this social since I was a teenager. Since I returned from Colorado, I only came into town when I needed to."

"Didn't you come in town to watch out for me?"

"Maybe at first, but now I realize how much I've enjoyed seeing people. They were all so good to me and Nate. And you'll be living here, too, so getting to know your neighbors would be nice for you."

Her arms tightened around the stuffed animals he'd won. She was having a lot of fun, but that didn't mean she needed to get so involved. "My life is a mess, Logan."

He pressed a finger against her lips as his green-eyed gaze held hers. "Let's just take it a day at a time and forget about everything for a little while."

She wanted to do that more than anything, but being around Logan and keeping her head on business was definitely a problem. She struggled not to give in. "Okay, but would you be hurt if I gave away some of these fellas?"

He put his hand over his heart. "I'm wounded. I worked hard to win all those great prizes."

She couldn't remember any guy doing this for her. "I'll keep this cute guy." She held up the sock monkey. "To remember all the fun we had today."

"I guess there might be some kids who would like to take the others off your hands."

They walked back to Main Street. Tori didn't have any trouble finding kids to adopt her pets. With her lone monkey in hand, they visited several craft booths. Tori ended up buying several raffle tickets for a beautiful Wedding Ring quilt. She then wandered to a woodworking booth and bought a 'Gone Fishing' sign to hang in the bunkhouse. Also some handmade jewelry for her sisters that she couldn't walk away from.

Hours later with her purchases and the sock monkey locked in the truck, Logan said, "Since you probably spent all your money, I'll buy dinner."

Tori opened her mouth to argue, but he shook his head to stop her protest. "Come on, I know a great food booth."

Logan took her hand and they walked back to the social and talked with more people who knew Colt as they waited in line for barbecue pork sandwiches served on crusty rolls.

Once at a table by the grandstand, Logan went off in search of a couple of beers. When he returned, Seth and Clara had joined them.

"I don't have to ask if you two are having fun," Clara said.

Tori smiled. "It's been a long time since I've been to a social. You were right, everyone here is so friendly. They all remember my father."

Clara nodded. "Your family settled here. Colt spent time here, too. And we're hoping that will keep you around. How's the bunkhouse coming? Are you ready to open?"

Tori took a bite of her sandwich, and swallowed. "Next weekend, that is if everything gets here. The new furniture, mattresses and chairs should arrive on Monday. And painter,

Juan's wife, Maria, agreed to cook breakfast for the guests."

Clara smiled and glanced at Logan. "Boy, you two have been busy."

Logan shook his head. "This is Tori's project. I'm just handling the ranching part."

"You're a good team," Clara said and stood. "I need to get back to work." She headed off through the crowd.

"Clara's right, Logan. You've helped a lot and I don't know what I would have done without you."

Logan glanced at Seth. He didn't deserve her praise. "What did I do? I gave you some names of people. I built a railing for the cabin, but that was something my grandfather would have done if he'd been around."

"You've agreed to run our cattle on your land."

"That's what neighbors do."

Seth joined in. "That's what neighbors do," he agreed with a smile as he stood. "I should get home. I need to load up early for a rodeo. Let me know when you want to move the herd."

Logan watched his friend walk off and wondered if he was really as okay as he let people think.

"Is something wrong?" Tori asked.

"Just concerned about a friend."

She smiled and took a sip of her beer. "I like Seth. I take he's single too."

"He was married once. Three years ago, he lost his wife, Ivy, and baby son in an automobile accident."

"Oh, God, that's terrible."

Logan nodded. He wasn't about to share the times Seth had tried to bury his pain in alcohol. "Seth's doing better. His rough stock business keeps him focused on something."

Tori touched his arm. "He's lucky to have a good friend to turn to."

"Seth would do the same for me."

"I'd say you're both pretty lucky."

They finished eating their sandwiches quietly and the band started tuning up for the first session. Logan went back for two more beers, but Tori insisted on paying this time, slipping him the bills.

When he returned with the filled plastic cups she took a sip. "I want to thank you for making today so much fun."

Logan figured that her ex had a lot to do with her not enjoying life. "Not a problem, we all need take time off."

She took another drink. "You've done so much to help me since I came here, there's no way I can ever thank you."

"We don't need to keep score." Logan wondered if she would still feel the same way when she learned that he'd put in a conflicting bid on her family's land.

Just then, the lead singer of the local band stepped up to the microphone and welcomed everyone, then began the first song. Several couples wandered out to the dance floor and started a quick two-step.

Logan didn't want to think about lease land, ex-boyfriends, or cattle. Today, he was just going to have a good time with a pretty woman. "I'm a little rusty, but would you like to dance?"

Tori frowned, her gaze flicking to the twirling couples and back to him. "It's been awhile for me, too," she admitted.

"Come on, let's take a chance." He stood and reached for her hand. She hesitated, but he managed to get her to the floor.

Logan took Tori in his arms and after a few stumbles, they were soon two-stepping like experts. Then the upbeat music ended and the tempo slowed to a ballad, the band began, a Garth Brooks' song, 'To Make You Feel My Love'.

Their gazes met as he drew her closer. He wrapped an arm around her waist and pressed her body against his, feeling her heat, her tempting curves. He placed his chin against her forehead and guided her into an easy rhythm around the floor.

Her intoxicating scent filled his nostrils, making him lightheaded with desire. His arm tightened against her back and he heard her sharp intake of breath. He groaned, trying not to make a fool of himself. When the music ended, he reluctantly released her. That was the last thing he wanted to do, but it was best if he kept his hands off her. Problem was that wasn't going to be easy.

***

The ride back to Colton Creek was quiet as Tori hugged her stuffed monkey to her chest. She didn't know how to handle her growing feelings for Logan. Feeling this way was crazy. She didn't need any complications, but how did she stop her attraction to the man?

Logan pulled up in front of the cabin. They sat there a second or two and she wondered what she should do. "Thank you again for the nice time, Logan. And for Jake." She held up the monkey, but that didn't stop him from leaning across the seat and drawing her toward him.

"Don't say anything." When he lowered his head toward hers, she didn't resist. She couldn't. He captured her mouth, tasting, nibbling and finally slipped his tongue inside.

She moaned and he pulled her against him, feeling his hard body. Her already sensitive nipples rubbed against his chest, and her breath caught in her throat. Her hands moved around his neck and let him deepen the kiss.

Finally he broke away. "I'm not apologizing for that, but hell, I can't say it was wise either." He moved back. "Come on, I've got horses to feed."

He climbed out of the truck before she even got a vote. Heart beat racing in her ears, she was glad someone had some common sense.

Once he came around to help her to the ground, she asked, "Would you mind if I visited Domino?"

"Sure, you can feed him."

She smiled. "I don't mind."

Once inside the barn, they went to work and concentrated on the horses, and not on the toe-curling kiss they'd shared just moments before. Tori filled Domino's feed bin.

"Hey, guy. Did you think we forgot about you?"

She was happy that the horse went right to his feed and began to eat. "That's it, boy. You eat it all up."

She leaned against the railing and saw Logan farther down the aisle feeding Buffy. She noticed how caring he was with the animals and they loved him. If she wasn't careful she would fall, too. She sighed. "Why can't life be easy, Domino? Why can't you meet the right person, fall in love and just live happily ever after?" She rubbed his mane, letting the coarse hair run through her fingers. "The big question is, will we ever be able to trust again?"

With one last pat on the gelding's head, she walked off to catch up with Logan. "You need me to do anything else?"

He shook his head, but his gaze didn't meet hers. "I think we're finished." He put away the buckets and turned off some of the lights. They started out of the barn, and Tori wasn't anxious to go to the cabin alone.

"I'll walk you up to the cabin," he offered.

She wasn't going to turn him down. "Thank you."

Once outside the barn, she noticed a light on in the bunkhouse. "I think the painters forgot to turn off the lights."

They headed in that direction, but when they approached the porch, Logan stopped and held out his hand. "The glass in the door is broken. Stay here."

Tori's heat pounded in her chest. This scene was all too familiar, reminding her of what had happened in her sister's townhouse.

"Oh, God, please be careful," she called as Logan walked to the door, pushed it open, and then turned on the overhead light. She heard him curse and she rushed inside. That was then she saw the freshly painted white walls. They were sprayed with words she couldn't repeat. Panic raced through her as she fought to hold back the tears.

"Let's go." Logan grabbed her hand and hurried her upstairs to his apartment on the second floor. He unlocked the door and they discovered the place hadn't been touched.

"You stay here and call the sheriff; the number is by the phone." He went into the bedroom and came out with his gun. Maybe he should have taken the weapon to the social. He definitely wanted to be armed now.

"Logan," she cried and he paused at the door. "Please, be careful."

Jaw clenched, he nodded and left.

With shaky steps, Tori went to the phone and called the sheriff. Tom Harris promised to come out to the ranch. After she hung up, she sank down in the chair and hugged herself, trying to control her shaking. There wasn't any doubt Dane had kept his promise and to come after her.

Oh, God. He wouldn't ever let her go. She'd never be free.

CHAPTER EIGHT

An hour later, Logan had gone through the entire bunkhouse, searching for any clues as to who did all this destruction. The walls needed to be repainted, and in the kitchen, the cabinet doors had been ripped off the hinges, and the dishes and glassware lay in shards on the floor.

The bedrooms weren't in any better shape with spray painted walls. In the bathrooms, both the mirrors and shower doors were broken.

"Damn. This is one sick dude," he murmured as he walked back to the main room. Through the window, he saw the flashing light of the sheriff's vehicle. Tom Harris got out and came to meet him at the door. He let the sheriff inside so he could see the damage himself.

The older man cursed. "This guy is seriously disturbed." He looked at Logan. "Where's Tori?"

"I had her stay upstairs."

"Not anymore."

They both turned and saw her come through the front door. She looked frightened, but mostly just sad. Logan wanted to go to her and assure her she would be safe, but he knew he couldn't guarantee her a damn thing.

"You don't need to be here, Tori," Logan said. "We can handle this, and the sheriff will come upstairs to ask you any questions he has."

"You don't have to protect me, Logan. I've seen Dane's anger and destruction before." She walked up to the disgusting message on the wall and her stomach soured. "This is definitely his work. He wrote the same message on my sister's wall."

She turned to face Tom Harris. "I'm sorry I spoiled your evening."

"Not a problem. It's my job to protect and serve this community." He took out a small notebook. "You say this is Dane Buckley's work?"

Tori felt tears well in her eyes, but she refused to let them fall. "It's the same message that was left in Josie's townhouse." She'd already told her sad, sick story to the sheriff earlier. This was exactly what she didn't want to happen when she came here.

"We might get lucky and he left something behind to incriminate himself."

Tori doubted that. "Well, no one has managed to catch him in the past two years."

Logan stepped up. "That was in a large city. We're rural here. Buckley might mess up and someone will see him around town."

"He could be headed back to LA already," she said.

The sheriff sighed. "Okay, I'm sending out a deputy to fingerprint the place in the morning, so leave everything as it is." With her nod, he looked at Logan. "Has anything else been tampered with?"

Reality hit, and Tori gasped. "Oh, God! The cabin." She ran out the door.

The two men hurried to catch up with her. Logan took the key from her as they went up the steps and he opened the door. Inside he turned on the light and both men walked around first, but she couldn't budge from the porch. *Please, don't let Dane damage the cabin.* She didn't want her ex to touch any part of her new home.

Logan came back to the doorway. "Okay, Tori. As far as I can tell, the place looks just as you left it," he told her. "You'll need to check for sure."

She nodded, unable to speak.

The sheriff came out to the porch. "I'll have my deputy check for prints here, too." He turned to Logan. "I take it you'll watch out for Miss Slater tonight." At Logan's nod, the sheriff headed back to his car.

Logan turned to her, his expression grim. "Grab whatever you need because you're staying with me tonight."

***

An hour later, Logan wasn't sure his suggestion was a good idea. He'd already spent the day with her. Now she was in his personal space, and he might never get her out of his system. He could blame the fact that he hadn't been with a woman in a long time, but he knew differently. The problem was all Tori. He only wanted her, but he couldn't let his feelings cloud his judgment. He had to focus on the man who was after her, get into his head and figure out the guy's next move. One thing for sure, he couldn't let this guy get to Tori.

"Logan..."

He turned from his seat at the desk to see the freshly-showered Tori. She was dressed in pajama bottoms and a tank top partly covered by a hooded sweatshirt. Her hair was pulled back into a ponytail, her face scrubbed clean. She looked tempting.

"What?"

"I'm too keyed up to sleep. Would you mind if I sit out here for awhile."

Definitely a bad idea. "Sure. You can watch television if you want. It won't bother me." He turned back to the computer. She didn't go to the sofa, but came and stood behind him as he searched the internet for anything about Richard Dane Buckley Jr.

Every breath he drew, he inhaled her scent. She'd used his soap from his shower, but the essence was pure Tori. When she leaned closer to read the screen, her breast brushed against his shoulder, nearly driving him to the edge. She pointed to something, but at this point he was losing all ability to concentrate.

Without thinking, he reached around and pulled her onto his lap, pressing his mouth against hers, his tongue quickly sweeping past her lips. He groaned as the heat of the kiss slammed through him, causing him to ache for more. His lips moved from her mouth to her throat, his tongue tracing the line of her collarbone.

"I need more of you."

Her eyes darkened with desire. "Logan…"

He parted her sweatshirt and ran his tongue along the edge of her tank top. This time she whimpered, and he covered her breast with his hand, quickly causing her nipple to harden against his palm. Then he moved to the other giving it the same attention. Wanting more, he tugged down her shirt, exposing her so he could take the hard tip into his mouth.

Tori arched her back as her fingers moved through his hair, holding him against her as she gasped his name. He pulled back and looked down at the beautiful woman in his arms. "Damn, you make me want things I have no business wanting." He leaned down and nibbled at her tempting mouth as he pushed her lower body against his erection. He groaned, and took one last hungry kiss then finally released her.

"We can't do this." He held her close as he drew several breaths, then he straightened her shirt and stood her up. With his last ounce of common sense, he got out of the chair. "You need to go to bed…alone."

Her shocked gaze made him question his decision, especially after seeing her soft and luscious body. His need was strong and he was weakening fast. “Please, Tori. I’m no good for you.”

A pink blush cover her face, she didn’t stop her from asking, “Why?”

He didn’t want to hash over his life. “My past. There are things that I’ve done.”

“There are things in my past, too.”

He managed a smile. “You might have picked the wrong man, but you’ve never done a bad thing in your life.”

She reached out her hand to touch him. “I don’t think you have either. Not the way you’ve been with me.”

He found how easy he could get lost in her. “Go to bed, Tori. I won’t be the man you need to comfort you tonight.”

She sucked in a sharp breath. He got what he wanted when she swung around and walked away. Problem was, how could he stop the ache he felt for her?

***

The next morning, Tori woke up when she heard Logan leave the apartment. She quickly got out of bed, wanting to be dressed and gone before he returned. The last thing she wanted to do was face him right now.

His rejection last night still stung. She made the bed, and stuffed her clothes into her bag, then grabbed her purse. Once down the steps she saw the deputy's patrol car and knew they were inside the bunkhouse gathering evidence.

That was another waste of time. Dane was clever enough to cover his tracks. She threw up a silent prayer, hoping Dane had made a mistake and left something behind to incriminate himself.

Logan came out of the bunkhouse and walked toward her. "Good, you're up. How did you sleep?"

She refused to look away. "I didn't."

His gaze locked on hers. "If it's any consolation, neither did I." He released a breath. "I apologize for last night. I should be whipped for taking advantage of the situation."

"You didn't hear me complaining." She glanced away. Darn, she still wanted this man. "I'm a big girl and I can take care of myself."

"I'm well aware of that. And you don't know how close I was to coming to your room and finishing what we started."

She opened her mouth to speak, but they were both distracted when the door to the bunkhouse opened and a deputy walked out.

Logan glanced over his shoulder to see Mike Abbott coming toward them. "Come on, let's see if they've found anything. Hey, Mike," he called to his old classmate from school. "Are you finished?"

He nodded. "But hold off going inside until I get the sheriff's okay first."

They stopped in front of the patrol car. "Mike, this is Tori Slater. Tori, this is Deputy Mike Abbott."

"Nice to meet you, Miss Slater," he said as they shook hands. "I wish we could have met under better circumstances."

"I wish the same, deputy. Please, call me Tori," she said.

"And I'm Mike." The deputy grew serious. "You take care, Tori. Seeing the condition of your place, this guy is pretty angry."

Logan saw Tori tense, and then she put on a smile. "I promise to be careful."

Mike drove off and Tori started toward the cabin. Logan caught up with her. He knew she was feeling to blame for this mess. "It's not your fault, Tori. You're not responsible for what Buckley has done."

She kept her head down and continued walking. "I shouldn't have led Dane on. Maybe if I hadn't moved in with him, if I hadn't made him so angry…"

He reached for her arm so she'd look at him.

She gasped and jerked away.

He immediately released her.

"Sorry." He held up his hands. "It's just frustrating to see what happens when these bastards get a hold of their victims."

When her eyes rounded, he said, "Yes, Dane made you a victim, Tori. He managed to control you for awhile, but you got out. Stop taking the blame for his actions."

Tears formed in those beautiful eyes of hers, but he couldn't stop speaking the truth. "Buckley took your trust, your independence and your love. He's the sicko." He reached out and, with a single finger, touched her cheek. "The good thing is, you got out, Tori. And I'll do everything I can to make sure that bastard never hurts you again."

"Maybe I should go back home to Montana," she suggested as she wiped away a tear.

His heart caught. She wanted to leave? "You could, and Dane might follow you there. And that would put your whole family in jeopardy."

She took a step toward him. Her dark gaze locked on his. "Logan, I don't want you to get hurt either."

He felt his chest tighten, that included his heart. "Damn, lady, you sure know how to turn a guy's head." He reached for her and drew her into his arms, then placed a kiss on her forehead.

"Logan, what am I going to do?" Her arms wrapped around his waist, and they just stood there. Nothing had felt this good in a long time.

"I can take care of both of us." He had to remember how much trouble he could get in when his feelings took over, but he was way past keeping this impersonal.

***

An hour later, Tori called her sister to let her know what had happened to the bunkhouse.

Josie had seen Dane's wrath in LA, so she could imagine the destruction.

"I think you should come home. Dane is dangerous and I don't want you hurt."

"No, if I give up now, we could lose everything. I believe we can make money from renting to anglers. But I need to delay the opening for another week and clean up. Maybe by then, Dane will make a mistake and show himself."

"I hate to think of you there alone."

Tori walked to the open cabin door and saw Logan putting the last of the pickets on the railing. Her heart fluttered when he paused and looked up at her. Quickly, she turned away. "I'm not alone, Josie. Logan is here."

There was a pause, then her sister said, "Hold on a second."

Then Tori heard another voice, "Tori, this is your father."

"Oh, hi, Colt."

"I'm sorry I left you such a mess there. I've neglected the Colton Creek."

"The conditions are not that bad." She went on to explain, "Nate and Logan have taken very good care of the place. The cabin is wonderful, and Logan has been fixing the porch."

"The ranch isn't as important as you are. You're not safe there, Tori. Josie's right, you should come home."

"I'm fine, Colt. Really. Logan is an ex-police officer. He knows how to handle this situation, and Sheriff Harris is helping, too."

"But this Buckley guy is unstable."

"Please, Dad." The thought of leaving made her heart ache. "I love being here in Rachel's cabin. I plan to dig deeper into research on our family and learn more about how they came to settle here."

There was a pause, then Colt said, "I have to say, it's been a long time since you sounded this happy."

"I truly love it here at the homestead." She also told him about all her plans for running organic cattle.

"Is McNeely around?"

"Yes, he's working on the porch."

"Good. Let me talk to him."

Tori walked outside to Logan and held out her cell phone. "Colt wants to talk to you."

Logan removed his work gloves and put the phone to his ear. "Yes, sir." He walked to the far end of the porch. Tori wanted to follow, but knew that if her father wanted her to know what they were saying, he would have told her. A few minutes later, Logan came back and handed her the phone.

"What?" she asked.

He shrugged. "Your father just wanted to know if I could handle the situation."

Great, that was all she needs. "Has he assigned you as my bodyguard? What's he paying you?"

Logan knew Tori would be upset, but Colt had every right to be worried about his daughter. "He didn't ask me to be your bodyguard and money never came up."

Tori sighed. “See, this is all getting out of hand. I should just take off where no one can find me, including Dane.”

She marched back into the cabin.

Before she could shut the door, Logan followed her inside.

“Look, Tori. I know this is hard on you. What’s it been, almost two years that this jerk has been after you?”

When she didn’t turn around, he went on. “You can’t let him get to you. That’s what he wants.”

“I just want Dane to go away and leave me alone. Maybe I can call his father. He can’t like his son causing bad publicity for their family.”

“People like the Buckleys couldn’t care less. I’ve known Sheriff Harris for a long time. The man will be relentless in finding Dane. Once his picture is shown around, everyone in town will be on the lookout.”

A gasp sounded then Tori’s hands covered her mouth. “Oh, God, now everyone will know.”

“Again, Tori, you have nothing to be ashamed of. Dane hurt you. He’s doing the damage, not you. And we’ll help you if you let us.”

Eyes brimming, she finally nodded. “Thank you.”

He smiled and coaxed one from her. “You’re welcome. How about we play hookey today and go riding? Maybe you can persuade Domino to go along.”

Those big eyes lit up. She had a real soft spot for the gelding. “You think he will?”

"I bet you can coax him out for a short trip." And Domino wasn't the only male drawn to her.

After locking up the cabin, Tori grabbed a hat and they walked out to the barn. After they saddled Buffy and Ace, Logan walked them out to the corral. Tori went to Domino's stall and attached a lead rope to his nylon halter. He immediately bobbed his head, but didn't pull back. One battle won. If only she could make other problems go away as easily.

"It's okay, fella, she said. "We're just going for a little walk."

She opened the gate and walked the horse out of the stall, then continued slowly out to the corral. With every step he took, she crooned to him.

When she saw Logan, she asked, "How am I doing?"

"Better than I did." Logan took both saddled horses and led them out the gate to the pasture.

Tori followed a little slower. "What happens if Domino panics and runs off?"

"We go after him and you can sweet-talk him back."

She rubbed Domino's head. "You seem to think I have a lot of influence with this guy."

Logan turned those deep-set green eyes on her and her pulse raced. "If you only knew," he said in a husky voice as he swung up onto Ace's back.

Tori climbed on Buffy, then she waited to see Domino's reaction. So far, he seemed okay with walking alone side the other horse.

"Let's go," Logan said and started off at a walk along the path toward the creek. Buffy and Ace fell into an easy stride alongside Domino.

Tori smiled. "I think they like each other."

"I'm picking up the pace," Logan told her and he started Ace into a trot.

Tori followed suit and Domino went right into the two-beat gait. "He seems comfortable with the pace," she said. "Good boy, Domino."

"Let out a little more rope," Logan suggested.

She did as he asked when they reached the open field.

"Okay, let's try a little faster." Logan took off into a three-beat cantor. Tori held her breath as she got Buffy to follow, and then so did Domino.

"Look at him, Logan. He's practically running and he's enjoying it."

Logan smiled at her. "He looks good but I don't want to push too fast right now."

About ten minutes later, they reached the wide creek, stopped and climbed down. The trees shaded them as they let the horses drink.

Logan watched Tori with Domino. She was a natural around horses and at home with ranch life. Most women he knew wanted to be in town, or in a big city.

"I know you said that you're never going back to LA, but will you move back to Montana when you get the rental going? I mean your family is there."

She sighed and glanced around. "I hadn't spoken to my father in years until six months ago. Even living in the same house during that time, things were still strained between us. I mean, I love him, but as for a relationship, we've never really had one."

Logan heard the emotion in her voice. "You said Colt wanted to change that."

"He might, but I'm not sure right now is a good time. Josie said he's investigating our mother's disappearance. Seems Lucia wants back into our lives, too."

Silently, Logan walked the horses to a tree and tied them to a thick branch. There was enough grass to keep the animals busy. He took a small rolled blanket from his saddle and laid it on the ground near a log. He sat, and then leaned back against the trunk.

"I can't tell you how to feel, Tori. I don't have any parents, and the last of my family died six months ago. So whatever chance I could have to find family, I would at least listen to the reason they left in the first place."

Tori walked to the blanket and sank onto her knees. "You can't imagine how badly I want to do that, but every time I've reached out, I've been pushed away."

He got the idea this conversation was going in a different direction. "You mean like I did with you last night?"

She managed a nod.

"I told you, I just didn't want to take advantage of the situation. You were frightened, you wanted comfort. I saw that in your face, in your get-lost-in-those-incredible eyes. I could see you wanted me, too. That's a heady stimulant for any man. I got sidetracked momentarily and I couldn't think past holding you in my arms, kissing you, having you in my bed."

Tori swallowed hard, feeling the tightening in her stomach. "What if I feel the same way?"

His gaze narrowed and his lips tightened into a straight line. "I'm not the settling-down type, Tori. I'm not the man you want me to be."

What woman did this to him? That was only one of the many things she wanted to know about this man. "Who was she, the woman who broke your heart?"

He stared for a long time. "Okay, maybe once there was someone special. Special enough that I was making plans for a future. I even trusted her with my life, and it nearly got me killed."

CHAPTER NINE

Why couldn't he just keep his mouth shut?

Logan shot to his feet and walked to the edge of the creek where the horses were grazing. Ace shifted in his direction, searching for attention. He reached out and rubbed the horse affectionately.

Tori came up behind him, but he didn't turn around. "I'm sorry, Logan. I had no business..." Her words trailed off.

He finally looked at her. "No one likes to rehash their mistakes, especially a mistake that cost me my career." *And so much more.*

Those dark bedroom eyes stared up at him. "You want to talk about it?"

He sent her a glare he hoped would end her questions. "Do you want to talk about Dane?"

Her gaze turned glossy with emotion. "If it would help you."

He wanted to tell her nothing would help him. "I'm well past crying on someone's shoulder. It's just your basic story. Faith chose someone else over me."

"How do you know? Maybe the situation just looked that way."

"Well, since she's dead, I can't ask her."

Tori gasped. "Oh, Logan, I'm sorry."

He shook his head. "I'm not sorry anymore."

"Of course you are, or you wouldn't be so upset. Someone you loved died."

"It wasn't like you think."

"Then what was it like?" she asked boldly.

She wouldn't stop until he told her the ugly truth. "Okay, Faith was whacked out on drugs when I first met her. I wanted to help her. Two years later, she'd gotten clean, had gone back to school and even reconnected with her family. We started dating. Seriously dating."

Tori remained motionless as Logan talked about the woman he'd nearly given up everything for.

"My job took me undercover, and I had to interact with some of the same drug pushers who'd hooked Faith. The main one, Denny Rodrigo, was a well known drug dealer. He'd also been Faith's dealer, or what I thought was past tense. Anyway, whether she knew it or not, she led me into a trap. Faith was killed and I was left for dead."

He looked up and saw the tears in Tori's eyes. "I'm sorry."

He shrugged it off as if the relationship hadn't mattered to him. But Faith's betrayal still stung. And the guilt he'd carried for the past three years reminded him he wasn't a good bet. "I'm over it. I came back here to Nate, and he got me involved in ranching again."

"That's where that scar on your side came from, isn't it" she asked.

"Yeah. Isn't having a permanent reminder convenient?"

She walked up to him and placed her hand against his side. "Does it still hurt?"

His heart accelerated as the heat of her palm seeped through his shirt, leaving him feeling edgy and off balance. "Not much anymore. I don't have time to think about it."

"I'm so glad you're okay. I don't want to think about you being hurt." He saw the tears fill her eyes, and his throat went dry. "Oh, God, you could have died..."

He reached for her and cupped her face. "Ssh. Don't, Tori. I'm fine, now." He never felt as alive as he did when she was in his arms. "Please, don't cry for me. I never should have let my feelings get in the way of my job."

"Faith betrayed you. She used you to get what she wanted, drugs."

"My mistake was I trusted her. I won't make that mistake again." He looked down at the woman he was growing more and more attracted to. "I can't, Tori. I don't have anything to give any more."

"I don't remember asking." She reached up and touched her mouth against his. Her lips were warm and inviting, and pulled at something inside of him that made him want more, making him need more of her.

"This isn't a good idea, Tori. I can't be the man you want me to be."

Those incredible eyes searched his. "You're a good man, Logan, but I won't ask for any more than this." Once again, her mouth met his. He tried to resist, but when she kept nipping and biting at his lower lip, he couldn't keep still. Damn the woman. She had no business barging into his life right now, messing with his head. Not now, not when he was so close to having everything he ever wanted. The ranch. But at this second all he wanted was her.

He grasped her arms, and pulled her closer. "Remember you asked for this," he told her, right before he crushed her mouth to his. There was nothing slow or gentle about the kiss, nor was his need for this woman. He'd been hungry for Tori Slater since the moment he laid eyes on her.

He drew her close and she melted against him. He went to the buttons on her blouse and opened her shirt. He cupped her lace covered breasts and she moaned as she pressed into his palms.

He broke off the kiss and looked her in the eyes. "I want you, Tori, so if you want to stop you'd better speak now, and we'll ride back."

Those midnight dark eyes stared at him. "I don't want to stop, Logan."

Grabbing her hand, he led her to the blanket and lowered her to the soft wool Indian print. Never taking his gaze off her face, he finished the job. "Ever since last night, I couldn't get you out of my head, and I need to touch you."

Tori laced her fingers in his hair and molded her body to his. This wasn't like her, but with this man she wanted to experience these new feelings. "I wanted you to come to my room," she breathed as she parted her lips, inviting his kisses.

"I nearly did. Now, I'm wondering why I fought so hard to get away," he told her.

Then his mouth claimed hers in a deep, drugging kiss, blocking out all her reasoning. Never mind that she'd only known this man a few weeks. That she swore she'd never get involved again. When he slowed the pace with lingering, wet kisses along her jawline to her ear, she nearly lost her mind as she pulled him back to her mouth.

She heard Logan's groan as her tongue ran along his lips and moved inside. He tore away his mouth, then made quick work of the front clasp to her bra and freed her small breasts. Her nipples immediately hardened even before he touched her.

"So pretty," he breathed. He drew her into his mouth and suckled gently.

At the sensation, she gasped in pleasure

He lifted his head and smiled. "And so responsive."

Tori looked up at him. She couldn't stop wanting him. She popped the snaps on his shirt, then moved her hand inside and touched his hard chest. That wasn't all that was hard. When he sucked in a sharp breath, she couldn't help but be pleased with herself.

Logan rose up on his elbows. "Be careful, you're playing with danger."

She'd never seduced a man in her life. Maybe now was that time. "What's going to happen?" she asked bravely.

"Whatever you want to happen. God, Tori, just don't stop."

She placed her other hand on his chest and continued the slow, agonizing exploration.

"You're killing me," he growled as his hand went to her jeans. "Two can play at this." He tugged down the zipper on her pants. All the time he was watching her, his green eyes reflecting his desire. He leaned down and placed open mouth kisses against her bare stomach and goose bumps rose on her skin.

She arched her back, wanting more from this man. "Please, Logan."

Fighting his own control, Logan reached inside Tori's panties and found her wet and ready. His heart slammed against his ribs as his fingers stroked her. He coaxed and encouraged her and within moments her release came. He captured her gasp of surprise in a searing kiss. When he broke off, they were both breathing hard, but he refused to let her go. When he looked down at her, she wouldn't meet his gaze.

"You're so beautiful," he told her, and leaned down and kissed her neck, then moved to feast once again on her luscious mouth when suddenly their privacy was disturbed.

Ace whinnied. Logan frozen and sensed they weren't alone. Sitting up, his cop instincts kicked in as he glanced at the area along the creek for any sign of Buckley. Instead he was relieved to recognize the horse and rider.

He glanced down at Tori questioning look. Hell, he let himself get distracted. Again.

Their perfect afternoon was about to end.

***

Thirty minutes later, Tori rode back with a silent, brooding Logan. When Seth had interrupted them, suddenly something changed with Logan. As if cold water had been thrown on them, making her feel very uncomfortable with what they'd just shared.

Tori took a chance to move past it. "You seemed angry that Seth caught us… together."

He glanced at her. "No, I'm angry I let down my guard. I need to be more vigilant with Buckley in the area."

The hurt began to disappear. "You regret us being together?"

For a long time he didn't say anything, then finally answered, "It's not that simple, Tori…" He paused. "I need to stay focused on your safety. Besides, you want us to be business partners, so getting involved isn't a good idea."

Tori straightened, trying to stay calm. “I’m not Faith, Logan.” She kicked her heels into Buffy’s sides and took off. She had to get away from this man before she strangled him. Finally, she reached the corral, and dismounted and led the mount into the barn. She was brushing Buffy when Logan led Domino and Ace into their stalls.

She glanced over to see him grooming Ace. His expert hands moved over the animal. She shivered, thinking about how those hands had felt on her. He knew just where to touch her. For the first time she knew what it was like to be cherished, to be put first, to feel such pleasure until you cried out. She looked at Logan. That experience had been only with this man.

He walked out of the stall and came close. “I’m sorry how the afternoon turned out, Tori.” He

took Buffy’s saddle from the railing. “If you don’t want to go back to the cabin alone, you can stay at the apartment.”

She had some dignity left. “I can deal with things on my own from now on. So I won’t be bothering you again.” She walked off, hoping Logan would call her back, but the barn was silent except for the sound of the horses.

Why did she always pick the wrong man? Once out of the barn, she quickened her pace across the compound until she finally was inside the cabin.

She sank against the door and looked around her new home. She wanted to stay here, but how could she when she was falling in love with a man who didn't want anything to do with her?

Okay, so another woman had hurt him. She'd been hurt, too. Yet, when it came to Logan McNeely, she had on blinders and fell hard. Well, the time had come for her to open her eyes.

Thinking about her great-great-grandmother, she walked across the room. "What would you do, Rachel? How did you get Cyrus to notice you, to fall in love with you? I bet you didn't let him cop a feel beside a stream."

Tori shivered at the thought of how Logan touched her, then drove her over the edge and into heaven. No wonder her sisters, Ana and Josie, looked so happy all the time.

She sank onto the sofa and closed her eyes. Would her life always be this way? Would she always be chasing a dream she could never have, a man she couldn't have? Would her memory only be of a man like Dane?

She sighed and walked to the cedar chest next to the fireplace. Maybe there were some more words of wisdom in Rachel's journal. She opened the lid and gasped when she saw the beautiful old quilt shredded into pieces. Suddenly, she began to shake. Oh, God. Dane. Was he here? Heart pounding, she turned as her gaze circled the room.

She jumped up, grabbed her purse and rushed to the door. She climbed in her car and raced across the compound. She jerked to a stop and jumped out as Logan walked out of the barn.

Breathing hard, she ran to him. "Dane was in the cabin."

"Stay here," he ordered and took off running.

Tori hugged herself, but the gesture didn't calm her, or stop the nightmare that just kept coming back.

***

Logan rushed through the door and then realized he didn't have his gun. He grabbed the twenty- two off the coat rack, made sure it was loaded, then went off on a search, checking room by room.

He wanted a chance at this guy so bad. Just a few minutes so he could remind the bastard how to treat woman.

Once he'd checked every room he stepped out to the porch to see that Tori had driven back in her car.

She climbed out, keeping a hand on the door. "Did you find anything?"

He shook his head. "What makes you think he's been here?"

"The cedar chest." She followed him inside. She then went to the chest and lifted the lid, exposing a quilt that had been cut up. She took out a handful of shredded fabric. "This had to be decades old." She leaned down, took out the journal and opened it to where she'd left off with her reading. She gasped.

He went to her. "What?"

She handed him the notebook. Written on a blank page was, *"We will be together soon, my lovely Vicki. D'"*

"It's the same handwriting as the letter," she told him. "How did he get in here?" She looked around, eyes widening and lips quivering. "Oh, God. He knew I read the journal. Dane is watching me."

Logan saw her panic and he couldn't blame her. "Well, he's not getting you. I need to call the sheriff." He moved away and pulled out his cell, not sure if this would do any good. This guy was daring to be caught. And Logan wanted to make that happen. But the best way to do that was to use Tori as bait, and he wasn't ready to do that.

He reported the incident to Tom Harris and put away his phone. "Pack up a few things and come to the apartment."

"I can't leave these things unprotected." A hand waved to encompass the cabin. "He's already destroyed a family heirloom."

"Tori, it's not worth your life. Buckley is risking everything to get to you. I'd say it's working." He took a step closer. "I won't let anything happen to you."

She looked at him, her eyes filled with tears. "Oh, Logan, I can't keep doing this. Someone will get hurt." She shook her head. "I don't want it to be you."

Hell, he couldn't resist her any longer and pulled her into his arms, telling himself he was only comforting her. "Oh, babe, Dane won't hurt me, and he won't hurt you, either. Not if I have anything to do about it. But I can't protect you if you don't let me."

"I can't leave Rachel's things here. Please, she's my family."

Seeing the truth in her words, he nodded. "Okay, then I'll move in here."

She started to protest, but he raised a hand. "I'll sleep down here. That way you'll be safe from the both of us." He turned and walked outside to check for any clues and keep away from temptation.

***

Later that day, the sheriff paid another visit and dusted for prints again. Two deputies had combed the area, looking for any sign of a strange vehicle around. There was nothing found to incriminate Dane.

By six o'clock Tori served up a roast and potatoes on a platter. Luckily, she'd planned ahead and she had put all the fixings in a slow cooker that morning before their ride. Before Logan nearly made love to her.

The sky was just getting dark when Logan walked back into the cabin. "I thought we told you to keep the door locked."

"I knew you'd be coming soon, but you're right. I won't do it again."

He walked to the kitchen counter. "Dane is so bold that would be all he needs. I have no doubt he gets his kicks from the fact he could get caught."

She shivered. "I don't want to talk about Dane anymore." She glanced at the table to make sure everything was set for their meal. "It's time to eat."

"I didn't expect you to cook for me."

She wanted to sock him. "I didn't just cook for you, I like to eat, too. But if you'd rather eat peanut butter and jelly, you can. I'm having roast and potatoes." She swung back to the counter and began carving the roast. Once the meat was on the platter, she carried it to the table, and then came back for the bowl of vegetables. Logan didn't speak until she took out the made-from-scratch biscuits out of the old oven.

"Maybe I am a little hungry."

She wasn't going to let him do this to her again. "Then you better wash up."

Logan wiped his hands on a towel as Tori poured iced tea into glasses. This arrangement wasn't going to be easy with her playing happy homemaker. He didn't need to be reminded of his solitary life. Not after today when he'd lost his focus and nearly made love to her. He couldn't let that happen again. Buckley was a serious threat and he couldn't let him get to Tori.

He went to the table and waited until she sat down, then he took the chair across from her.

"This looks good."

"Well, there's plenty of food, so don't be shy."

He picked up the meal platter and took three slices of beef and several potatoes. He glanced up and saw her smiling. "You said to eat. And since meals like this aren't waiting for me most nights,

I'm going to take advantage." He took a bite and moaned. "This is delicious," he told her, his mouth full of food.

"I love to cook. I just don't have much of a chance, and it's hard when I'm the only one eating."

"Maybe you should offer meals for the anglers."

"The recipe's pretty simple. Just put all the ingredients into a slow cooker and let it go all day." Grinning, she lifted her fork with a slab of meat. "And this is the result."

Logan took another bite of the savory meat. It was so good and only one of Tori's many talents. What man wouldn't want her in his life? Too bad she kept choosing the wrong man. It wasn't him, either.

"I'll think about doing that," she told him. "Right now, I need to get the bunkhouse repainted."

This was when he needed to add a little advice. "Might be better to hold off a few days and see what develops."

She couldn't hide her fear, not from him. "You think Dane will come back, don't you? Of course he's coming back. And he'll keep doing things until I figure out a way to get him out of my life."

"We'll apprehend him, Tori." He didn't mention they would need a confession admitting to the break-ins. They had to make sure Buckley's daddy couldn't get him off again.

He watched her push her food around on the plate, then finally set down her fork. "You can't guarantee that. If I relocate somewhere else, then maybe he'll leave you alone."

His grip on his fork tightened. He couldn't believe she was worried about him. "I can take care of myself. Who will protect you? Stop worrying about everyone else." He sucked in a breath and lowered his voice. "Dane wants you, and to hell with what you want."

"But you're in his way."

"That's right, and I'll stay in the way, until we get this guy. Buckley won't hurt you again."

He could see she wanted to say something, but instead gave a nod and went back to her food.

Forty minutes later, supper ended and they both cleaned up the dishes. Then Tori went to work on her laptop at the counter while Logan flipped through the channels on the small flat-screen television. Not that he was interested in watching anything, he just needed a different focus other than Tori. Their close quarters the past two nights had been playing havoc with his libido. Oh, hell. Tori Slater had played havoc with everything he'd once thought he could live without.

***

The next morning, Tori had to get away from the cabin. Since Dane again invaded her sanctuary, she couldn't stand to stay there alone. Logan had spent about an hour contacting a security company to have lights and cameras installed in the cabin, bunkhouse and surrounding outbuildings.

Then she followed Logan out to the barn and visited with Domino. She even managed to coax the black gelding out into the corral. Once in the ring, he wanted to run. He took off and circled the arena, making Tori smile.

"Well, look at you, fella," she said, wondering how she would catch him. Surprisingly, she called his name and he came to her. He nudged her, and she rubbed his face and fed him a carrot. "So now that you've had some freedom, you want more, huh?"

The animal bobbed his head and she continued to give him attention. Then as if a game, Domino took off running toward the other end of the corral, then he'd come back. She could see that he waited at the gate.

"Sorry, boy," she spoke softly. "I can't let you out." She looked around for Logan and spotted him busy stacking hay bales. "I wouldn't mind running away with you, boy." Domino whinnied again, sounding more insistent.

Tori pressed her face against the animal's back, her hand rubbing over his scarred coat, reminding her of the pain he'd gone through. Her heart went out to the once-abused animal. "Would you even let me on your back? And how would I get there?"

She glanced around, saw the large water trough and led the horse there. "Okay, but you better not buck me off, or I won't be happy."

Domino swung his head around to look at her. She could swear he understood her. "Yeah, I'm the crazy one. I haven't ridden bareback since I was about twelve."

She got the horse positioned, then, with the lead rope in hand, she climbed on the edge of the trough. With crooning words, she grabbed hold of the animal's mane and pulled herself up onto his back.

Immediately, Domino danced sideways. "Whoa, fella. It's okay, it's only me," she said, keeping her voice even. "I won't hurt you." She rubbed her hands over his back until the animal calmed, then she took command and it felt good.

Logan walked out of the barn and spotted the horse and rider. Domino? He froze suddenly afraid for Tori, but he stood back and watched the twosome.

She took control of the gelding with just her legs and her gentle hands on the reins. Her manner was as if they'd ridden together a long time--and she was bareback.

He pushed back his hat. "Well, I'll be dammed."

Once more, she circled the corral and looked over at him and smiled. "Can you believe it? Isn't he wonderful?" she crooned.

Why was he jealous over the attention she gave a horse? "That's pretty good."

She came to a stop in front of him. "We've been going around and around for the past twenty minutes. He really wants to run, but I'm not leaving the corral without a saddle."

"That's good to know." He glanced at her slim legs that hugged the horse's sides. She looked damn good sitting there. "Ok, what kind of magic did you use to have him let you on his back?"

She gave him a smug look. "That's my secret."

He shook his head. "You're one hell of a horsewoman."

She shrugged. "I'm Colt Slater's daughter. He was a rodeo champion. It's in my blood."

His attention moved up to her face. "I can't believe you lived in LA all those years."

Her smile disappeared. "A mistake I'm regretting now."

She grabbed a handful of mane, and started to dismount, but Domino decided to shift away. Logan moved fast and was there to catch her. As if an instant replay, he was reminded of earlier and how she felt in his arms. She paused as he lowered her to the ground. He didn't want to let her go, but he had no choice. If he took this attraction any further, she could get hurt.

Tori had other ideas. She turned in his arms, then slid her hand up his chest and around his neck. He felt the heat as her touch grew bolder, and her body pressed against his. Then her mouth was tempting him with teasing bites.

Then he didn't care about anything except how much he craved her, her mouth, her body. She made him realize how empty his life truly had been.

At his back, he felt a sharp nudge and broke off the kiss. Domino wanted to make his presence known. He whinnied, showing his possessiveness.

Tori's laugh kicked his arousal up a notch. *God, this woman is going to kill me.*

With a grin, she turned back to him. "Sorry, seems my guy here needs some attention." She grabbed the lead rope and walked away, leaving him standing there, aching to go after her.

CHAPTER TEN

Around midnight, lightning flashed across the sky outside Tori's bedroom window. Seconds later, thunder vibrated through the old cabin as rain beat against the metal roof, startling her awake.

As lightning lit the sky once again, she jerked up. Pulling the sheet against her body, she leaned against the headboard as a boom of thunder reverberated around her, sound like it ringed the valley several times. After living in LA, she'd forgotten about the extreme weather of this area. One of many things she hadn't missed.

Another flash of light caused menacing shadows across her walls, then another loud thunderclap crashed and she jumped. She knew Dane couldn't get to her with Logan downstairs, but that still didn't stop her heart from racing. Then the big tree outside brushed against the house, making a scratching noise. That did it. Getting up, she wrapped herself in a robe and headed downstairs. The sofa was where she would spend the rest of the night.

Tori came down the steps into the dark area. The only light was over the stove in the kitchen. She glanced toward Logan's room and found the door open. Oh, boy, how badly did she want to climb into bed with him? Another flash of lightning and she found herself scrambling to his doorway.

Then if things couldn't get any worse, she heard a gun's safety being released.

"Whoever you are, you have about two seconds to identify yourself."

"Don't shoot, Logan. It's me, Tori."

Then she heard his familiar curse. She hated that everything she did or said seemed to irritate him so much.

Logan wanted the intruder to be anyone but her. He put the safety back on his Glock and set it down on the table beside the bed. He got up and went to her. "What's wrong?"

"I can't sleep." She stepped through the doorway, eyeing his lack of clothing. What did she expect, he had on pajamas bottoms.

"What is it?" he asked.

"The storm… I keep seeing shadows on the walls. I keep thinking it's Dane."

She moved closer.

Logan caught her scent and arousal hit him. His body reacted immediately and he groaned.

"Can I stay down here with you?" she asked.

He hissed out a breath. "Tori... that's not a good idea."

"I promise you won't even know I'm here." Lightning flashed again and she jumped.

He should go sleep on the sofa, but something told him that she didn't want to be alone.

"Tori, it's okay. It's only a thunderstorm."

"The bed is big, and I don't take up much space." She pointed to far side of the bed. "I'll sleep over there."

"Ah, Tori... You know what's going to happen if you climb into this bed."

She raised her head and with the aid of lightning flashes he saw the longing in her eyes. "You're right, I shouldn't have bothered you."

She started to turn away, but he reached out and stopped her. "Don't, Tori. You know the only reason I'm sending you away."

"Okay, I'll go sleep on the sofa."

"No, you take the bed, I'll bunk on the sofa."

Before either of them could move, there was a crash and the sound of glass breaking upstairs.

"Oh, God. What was that?"

"I don't know, but I'll find out." He reached for jeans and pulled them on along with his boots. Then he grabbed his gun. "You stay here," he told her.

With her nod, he took off. Not turning on any lights, he crossed the main room of the cabin, then took the stairs two at a time and he stopped at Tori's bedroom. He cautiously looked inside to see the strong winds had broken a tree branch and it came through the window.

Great, just what he needed. He put his gun down on the dresser and went to assess the problem. As the blowing rain poured in, soaking the floors, he worked on removing the broken tree limb, then shoved it back outside.

The window was a total loss. He went to the hall cabinet and found a plastic shower liner for a temporary fix. Hurrying downstairs to get his toolbox, he found Tori waiting for him in the kitchen.

His jaw clenched. "Why are you out here?"

"I was worried about you."

"How can I protect you when you don't listen?"

"I promise I'll do what you ask. What broke the window?"

"A tree branch came through your bedroom window. I'm covering the opening until morning." He went to his tools beside the door and grabbed his hammer and nails. "Go climb into bed, and I'll be back in a few minutes."

He made the temporary fix, knowing Tori couldn't come back even if she wanted to. He wiped the rain from his face and upper body, then went downstairs and to his room, to Tori. And damn if it didn't excite him as he opened the door and found her standing beside the bed.

"Logan?"

He was crazy to even think about getting involved with her, but God help him he couldn't resist her much longer. With the thunder rumbling through the room, he reached out to reassure her, but somehow she was in his arms, a combination of sweet and sensual. Good Lord, he was only human.

"You can't go back upstairs even if I wanted to send you, which I don't."

He felt her trembling, and this time he doubted the reaction was from the storm. "I don't want to leave you, either," she told him in a whispered voice.

With her hands on his chest, he lost all conscious thoughts and desire hit him like a punch in the gut. He had to have her.

"God, Tori, I want you." He met her gaze. "But this still isn't a good idea because I can't offer you anything but here and now. The smartest thing to do would be for me to turn around and get the hell out of here."

When he didn't budge, she answered, "I want you, Logan." Then she took his hand and led him to the bed.

This wasn't good, not good at all, he chanted as the rain pounded against the window, surrounding them in a private world. The lightning flashed and thunder boomed across the sky as he prayed Buckley wouldn't come out in this weather.

"God, Tori, I want you, too." Standing next to the bed, he cupped her face and kissed her. There wasn't anything hesitant about the way he took her mouth, the kiss was hot and hungry. His hands moved over her body, and the thin sleep shirt did little to hide her curves. He went from her waist up her ribs to cover her small, firm breasts. A perfect handful.

She moaned against his mouth, testing his patience which was pretty much gone. He broke off the kiss and stripped off her robe. He immediately reached out and touched her, then kissed the rigid peaks through her thin T-shirt, then pulled down the fabric and eagerly laved each nipple with his mouth.

"Oh, Logan. Please..."

"Please what, Tori?" He paused and waited for her to make the next move. "Feel free to take what you want from me."

Tori tried to ease her breathing as she worked to push aside the pain of her past out of her head. All that mattered was this time right now with this incredibly sexy man. She placed her palms against his chest, relishing the hardness of his muscles, and the sleekness of his skin under her fingers.

She looked up into his eyes. "I'm not sure if I can please you..."

He huffed out a laugh. "All you have to do is just stand here and it's almost more than I can handle."

Given sudden courage, she began to move her hands over his heated skin. He was beautiful. She raked her fingers through the dark hair swirling around his small flat nipples. He drew in a sharp gasp and she smiled, then surprised herself when she leaned close, replacing her fingers with her mouth, using her tongue to please him.

With a curse, he raised her face to his and devoured her mouth, driving his tongue past her lips. Blood pounded in her ears, and she moaned as the sensations ran deep down into her stomach and lower. He lifted her up so she could feel his hardness against her. She broke off the kiss and gasped. "Logan, I've never felt like this."

"Just wait, darlin'" he promised as he laid her down on the bed, and stretched out beside her. "We're just getting started."

She hesitated. "Yesterday when you touched me… I've never done… it was wonderful." With gentle fingers, she touched his face. "Thank you."

Logan fought to keep control. He would find Buckley and hurt him if it was the last thing he did.

"Let's see if we can get past wonderful."

Logan cupped her face and kissed her mouth, savoring each taste of her, each sweet response. He wanted to keep things slow and easy, but doing so was damn difficult. And he was about at his limit.

"First, let's get out of the rest of these clothes." He pulled her T-shirt over her head. Placing her sweet breasts in the palm of his hands, he used his finger and thumb to tease the nipple.

Tori seemed to sense the growing torment, and she reached for him. "Oh, Logan."

He took control when he nudged her lips apart, and she whimpered and welcomed him inside.

He continued his hungry assault along her jaw and neck, and then tugged down her pajama bottoms, taking her panties with them. Unable to resist, he leaned and kissed her flat stomach. She sucked in a long breath as goose bumps rose against her heated skin. He returned his attention to her mouth as he pressed his body to hers, needing the contact more than his next breath.

He shifted his hands down to the inside of her thighs and began to explore her smooth skin. He found the heart of her and slipped inside to find her ready for him.

"Please, Logan. Make love to me."

"Damn straight I will, and nothing will stop us this time."

He stood, went to his duffle bag on the dresser and took out his shaving kit. After taking out a condom, he slipped it on and returned to her side of the bed.

He leaned down and began to kiss her slow and easy, and then quickly deepened it as his attention moved to her breasts and back to her mouth as he rose over her. Slowly, he eased himself into her, inch by painstaking inch until he filled her. And she filled him, too, all those empty spaces in his soul. As the tempo increased, her eyes locked with his.

He had to fight the overwhelming sensations and concentrate on Tori's pleasure. Then she gasped, her hands clamped on his back, and he felt her tighten around him. He flew off to heaven as wave after wave moved through him. He reached down and covered her mouth, unable to put into words the feelings coursing through him. He rolled over and pulled her with him. He wasn't ready to let her go. Maybe he never would be.

***

Tori woke up before dawn to discover the rain had stopped and Logan's arm was across her chest, his body pressed against hers. She sighed and stared up at the beamed ceiling and felt the steady rhythm of his heartbeat. It had been so long since she'd let anyone get this close. And she'd never experienced true intimacy, the complete and total connection shared between two people. She smiled. She never suspected someone like Logan McNeely would be such a sweet and tender lover.

Heat crept up her body, as she recalled what she'd shared with Logan. A man she'd known for barely three weeks. Less than a month and she'd already fallen hard, head over heels in love with this man. The realization startled her but not enough to make her regret last night.

She glanced at the bedside clock. In a few hours she had to return to reality. She wasn't giving up one precious second of time with Logan. She tilted her head and looked at her lover. His dark beard covered his wide jaw. His mouth was perfect, the bottom lip was fuller than the top and he sure knew how to use them.

"Like what you see?"

She shifted her gaze to find Logan had one eye opened and those incredible lips twitched into a smile.

A blush rose in her cheeks. “Very much.” Over the past eight hours, she had grown bolder. She leaned forward and placed random kisses along that stubborn jaw, then moved down his chest.

He made a low rumbling sound as he rolled onto his back. “I need to fix that window and check for water damage.” He groaned and his hands ran up and down her back. “Good thing I got up earlier and fed the horses.”

She raised her head and smiled, feeling his growing desire. “So I might persuade you to stay in this warm bed a little longer?”

The look he gave her was nothing short of a leer, and her belly quivered.

“Maybe.”

An hour later, sated and nearly giddy, Tori reluctantly let Logan slip out of bed. In the dim light, she watched as he crossed the room, loving the chance to steal a glance at his gloriously naked body. He grabbed some clean clothes from his bag, and announced he was taking a shower.

She almost asked to join him, but caught his distracted look. “I need to replace the window in your bedroom, and the security people are coming out.”

She tossed a pillow at him. “Go away. I don’t want to come back to reality yet.”

When he turned serious, she wondered if he was regretting last night. “Don’t look at me like that, Tori, or I’ll forget all my good intentions and climb back into that bed.”

“Would that be so bad?”

"Yeah, it would. Buckley's out there and we still need to be careful."

For an instant, her body tensed. She didn't want her ex to intrude on their special time together. "Okay, but last night was wonderful."

"Not denying that. And it would be so easy to let your sexy little body distract me." He tossed her PJ's onto the bed. "So help me out here and put on some clothes."

She smiled and slowly slipped into her top and pants. "How about I fix breakfast?"

"That would be great."

She started past him and he reached for her and covered her mouth with his. Within seconds, things took a turn from sweet to sensual. When he finally broke off the kiss they were both breathing hard. He studied her for several seconds and tucked a strand of hair behind her ear. "You're a cruel woman, sending me off to a cold shower." He caressed her cheek then turned and walked into the bathroom.

Dear heaven, she had to use a lot of willpower not to follow him. Instead Tori went into the kitchen, took bacon out of the refrigerator and placed it in the skillet. She had the table set and orange juice poured, when there was a knock sounded on the door.

She tensed. Who could that be at seven in the morning? She worked to remain calm as she peered out the window and saw the familiar truck with Montana license plates.

She tied the belt on her robe, unlocked the door and opened it to find Colt Slater standing on the porch. "What are you doing here? Is something wrong back home?"

With his hat in his hand, Colt Slater stepped across the threshold. "All's fine back home. I'm here because my daughter is in trouble."

The older man walked past her into the cabin.

Great. Now, she had her father to deal with.

She turned to see him looking around the living area. "Just for the record, I'm not in trouble."

His startlingly blue eyes met hers. "Okay, bad choice of words, but you can't deny there's a crazy bastard after you."

Something inside her loved that her father wanted to take care of her. For the first time in years, he was making an effort. But could she trust him after a lifetime of neglect? "And the sheriff here is handling it."

"I know, I talked to him last night when I arrived in Dawson Springs. I would have come out then but the storm stopped me."

She tried not to react. Dear Lord, if he'd come out any earlier he might have interrupted more than breakfast.

"Tori, did Dane do something else?"

"No. We haven't seen him at all." She caught a whiff of the bacon burning and hurried back to the kitchen. "Can I make you some breakfast?"

"No, I ate earlier in town. But I wouldn't turn down more coffee."

She watched the man with the thick gray hair. He stood just under six feet tall. His body was trim and looking strong for someone of fifty-four.

So different from a few months ago when he was still recovering from a severe stroke.

He sat at the table and glanced at the place setting with a quirked eyebrow. "So where is McNeely?"

Oh, boy. She didn't need this. "He's in the shower. Since Dane broke into the cabin, Logan has been staying here."

Those piercing blue eyes, those Slater blue eyes stared back as he rose from the table.

"What? You're the one who asked him to watch out for me. So he is staying in the cabin." She wasn't doing this very well.

Colt moved around to the other side of the counter and sat again. He had a feeling that he should've called ahead before he just barged in on his daughter. The last thing he wanted to do was play over-protective father, but that was exactly what he felt like doing.

"Look, I'm not here to tell you what to do, Tori, I'm just worried about your safety." He hesitated, finding an explanation hard. He had to try if he wanted to win back his daughter. "I know I haven't been the best dad in the world, but I'm here now."

Suddenly she heard the bathroom door opened and Logan walked out from the hallway, pulling his shirt over his head. "I hope you fixed me extra eggs, I worked up an appetite." When the shirt was all the way on, he saw Colt.

He nodded. "Mr. Slater." He walked over and reached out his hand. "Good to see you again."

Colt stood and shook it. Yes, definitely something was going on between them. "Sorry to just drop in, but I was worried about Tori. Ah hell, the truth is, I needed to get away from the Lazy S for awhile."

Tori stepped close to the men. "Driving to Wyoming is a long trip. What if you had another... had trouble?"

Good, she was worried about him. "My doctor gave me the okay to travel, so stop fretting over me. I could have stayed home with your sisters for that."

She nodded. "Then there must be another reason you showed up. Is it because you don't think I can handle the job here?"

"Stop putting words in my mouth, young lady. I told you, I came because I was worried about that lunatic running around. Is it so awful to care?"

He watched Tori blink back tears. "If that's why you're here."

He glanced at Logan. "It's part of it. But why don't we eat breakfast and catch up first?"

"Just so you know, Colt, I'm not going back to Montana. I'm staying here."

Colt smiled. He could say one thing about his daughters; they weren't afraid to speak their minds. "I wonder where you got your stubbornness from."

***

By noon, Logan had shown Colt every inch of Colton Creek, and answered dozens of questions. The window company had replaced the glass pane in Tori's bedroom and the broken remains had been cleaned and disposed of. He needed to keep his distance from her. At least until he sorted out his own problems. Damn, Colt showing up and cooling things off was probably a good thing.

As they walked back through the barn, he wanted to know the real reason for the older man's impromptu visit. "Okay, now it's my turn. What are you really doing here?"

Colt paused next to Domino's stall. Logan had already explained about the problems with the horse. Yet the man managed to get the animal to come to him. The ability must run in the family.

"It's mainly what I said. I want to make sure Tori is okay. And I can see you have things under control."

When he paused, Logan waited, vaguely aware that a horse stomped a hoof in another stall.

Finally Colt said, "The other reason I'm here is Tori's mother. She's reappeared in my life after a long absence. Tori already knew about Lucia contacting me when she volunteered to come here, but I wanted to tell her about some new developments."

Logan didn't like the idea of piling on more stuff for Tori to deal with. "Is the news something that will upset her? Because I think she has enough to handle with Buckley right now."

The lines around Colt's eyes crinkled. "It's not that easy, son. I don't want her to be left out, or hear the news from someone else." Colt hesitated, then leaned against the stall. "You see, Lucia has been gone for a lot of years. We learned recently she hadn't been given a choice. She had to leave to protect the family."

"And of course, you believe her?" The words came from a familiar voice.

Both men turned to see Tori standing within earshot.

With hands fisted at her side, she walked to them, directing her anger at Colt. "Your memory seems to be pretty short, so I'll remind you. She never said goodbye. *All those years ago* when she left us, we never had a word from her. Marissa was barely a year old. How can you forgive her for that?"

Colt stood his ground. He knew this would come up, but it was good they clear the air. "Because your mother had no choice but to leave us," he argued. "I've paid an investigator to go to Mexico and learn the truth about her disappearance all those years ago."

Colt saw Tori's sadness, but he didn't need to be involved in this.

"I should go," Logan said.

"No!" Tori said, reaching for him. "Please, stay, Logan. You probably know most of our family history anyway."

Colt nodded his okay, and then began. "It's true, Tori, your mother left me when you all were just babies. What you don't know is that Lucia was forced to leave because a drug lord, Vincent Santoya, threatened to kill all of us if she didn't do what he said."

"And why would some drug lord come to Montana to find a woman?"

Colt knew the story sounded made up, but it was true. He just had to make his daughter believe it too. Their future as a family depended on her acceptance. "I know the details sound farfetched, but when your mother was barely a teenager, her father had promised her in marriage to Vicente. Her family, the Delgados, had been involved in illegal activities, too."

Colt pushed away from the stall and walked along the center aisle to his daughter. "Everything Lucia told me was verified by my P.I. when he found the remaining Santoya family and your mother's family. And since Vicente's death, she was free to come back to us."

Tori's expression softened.

Colt felt a surge of hope. "Why couldn't she have contacted us in all those years? Tell us that she loved us, that she would come back as soon as she could?"

"Communication was too dangerous. Mainly too dangerous for her sons, our sons," Colt clarified. "You have brothers, Tori, Rafael and Quintin."

"What?" Tori looked at Logan, and then back at her father. "I can't deal with this."

She started to turn away when Colt called her name. She put up her hand. "Not now, Dad. I can't do it."

Her voice trembled with emotion, and she hurried off. Colt started after her, but Logan stopped him. "Sir, maybe you should let her go."

Colt turned to the younger man. He suddenly felt old and tired. "I know, but she's hurting so much. I truly came here because I was worried about her. Damn, I never should have said anything about her mother. I just want her to know that I love her. God, I pray it's not too late to prove it."

CHAPTER ELEVEN

By the afternoon, the trees outside Tori's bedroom window had been trimmed back away from the house. When the security company showed up, Logan supervised the placement of the cameras and that project kept Colt busy, too. Good. For the moment, she didn't have to deal with her father.

So she concentrated on cleaning her bedroom, then she went downstairs and stripped the sheets from the bed, smelling her lover's scent. She tried not to relive the picture of her and Logan's night together. The real question was, how did he feel about her after what happened? Since her father showed up practically at dawn, she hadn't had a chance to speak with Logan. She tugged on fresh pillowcases, and then placed the pillows against the headboard.

Her feelings for the solitary rancher were even stronger than before, but she had a suspicion the man was pulling back.

She drew a breath and released it. Why would Logan want to get involved with her anyway? She had an ex-boyfriend who was stalking her, a father she had issues with, and a failing family ranch. Yeah, why would a guy want to jump right into the middle of all that?

Except for one thing, last night with Logan had made her feel things she'd never felt before. As if she finally fit somewhere, right here at the Colton Creek with him. Not the best time to finally meet that one great guy… or to fall in love, but that was what she'd done.

After airing her dirty laundry, she couldn't blame Logan if he thought she was too much trouble. No doubt Colt had been giving him the third degree, too.

She pulled the faded quilt over the big bed and gathered up the soiled sheets from the floor, then put them in the hamper in the bathroom. Not eager to face Dane's sick destruction, she'd take them down to the washer and dryer in the bunkhouse another time. She was glad the painters were scheduled to return tomorrow and clean up the mess. Then maybe things would get back to normal. Would Dane let that happen? Would he ever get tired of stalking her? And would her father return to Montana and let her run the operation here? She was doubtful on both counts.

She walked into the kitchen and thought about supper. Not able to make a trip into town for more supplies, leftovers would have to do.

Tori's meal prep was interrupted by a knock on the cabin door. She felt her heart start to race, knowing the cameras weren't hooked up yet.

"Who is it?" she called, eyeing the shotgun on the rack on the wall.

"Clara Williams."

Tori quickly opened the door to the general store's proprietor.

"Oh, Clara. Hi."

The woman smiled. "Hello, Tori."

Tori motioned her inside. "This is a surprise." Clara was dressed differently. Instead of her usual western shirt and jeans, she had on a pretty pink sweater and charcoal slacks. Tori couldn't help but wonder if the woman's visit had anything to do with Colt's arrival in town.

"I hired my nephew, Tom, so I can take a few hours off," the older woman told her. "A person can't work 24-7, you know. Speaking of which, you haven't been in town since the spring social." She frowned. "I heard about the vandalism. I'm so sorry, Tori." She shook her head. "I'm still struggling to believe something like this can happen in our community."

Tori didn't want to divulge the incident had to do with her poor choice of men. "Logan is installing security lights and deadbolt locks."

That brought back the older woman's smile. "He's a pretty good guy to have around."

Oh, boy. She didn't want to get Clara started again. "So, what brings you out here?"

Clara smiled as she held up a beautiful blue and cream colored quilt. "You won the raffle."

Tori felt her spirits soar. "Really? I won this?"

Clara nodded. "And it's Hattie Pickard's, too. She's one of the best quilters in these parts. It's not only beautiful, but will last for years." Clara spread the coverlet out on the back of the sofa. "You can hand this down to your children."

Tori looked over the intricate details of the gorgeous design, and something struck her as odd. This wasn't the double wedding ring quilt she'd bought a ticket for. "Not that I'm complaining Clara, but are you sure this is the same quilt?"

Clara shrugged. "I wouldn't know because I hadn't seen it before I offered to bring it out here."

Tori looked at her and felt emotions clog her throat. Had Clara heard about the shredding of Rachel's quilt, and decided to replace it herself? "That's your story and you're sticking to it?"

The older woman nodded. "Damn straight." Then she grinned. "You know if you ever need anything, Tori, all you have to do is ask. We take care of our own."

Holding back her emotions, Tori hugged her. Since their first meeting, she'd felt a closeness to this woman. "You are so sweet, Clara Williams."

Clara pulled back. "Don't let the word get around, okay? A woman in business has to be tough to play with the big boys."

"Your secret is safe with me. Would you like to stay for supper?" Tori tried to gather back words, remembering her father. "First, I need to tell you Colt arrived this morning."

The older woman sobered. "I heard rumors he was in town. How is he doing?"

"Stubborn as ever, but he's feeling well enough to drive all the way here to check up on me." She hesitated. "Clara, I don't know how close you two were over the years and it's none of my business, but I don't want you hurt. My father brought me news about my mother. Seems she's shown up at the Lazy S."

A flash of pain appeared in Clara's pretty hazel eyes. "Why would I care?" She paused, sighed deeply then said, "Am I that obvious?"

"No. But Logan told me he remembered you were good friends with Colt." She raised a hand. "And there's nothing wrong with that. My parents were divorced years ago. I'm guessing you were deeper in the relationship than my father."

She shook her head. "I can't say the man didn't warn me. Colt didn't want anything permanent."

Tori felt a sudden stab of pain. Hadn't Logan told her the same thing? "Isn't that typical of a man? They're so afraid we're trying to tie them down."

"Yeah, and most of them aren't even house broke."

Both of them laughed, and then Clara sighed. "So you have to be happy your parents are back together."

Tori didn't want to air anymore of the Slaters problems. "I haven't seen my mother in over twenty years, Clara. So I don't remember her much. And since I've been living here, I'm still not sure what's going on in Montana." She would let her sisters sort out the facts.

Before Clara could say anything more they heard the sound of boots on the porch floor. The door opened and Logan and Colt walked in. They stopped on seeing Tori's guest.

No one spoke for what seemed like forever, then Colt walked across the room and removed his hat. "Hello, Clara." His blue eyes softened, and he reached for her hand. "It's been a long time."

***

Logan watched Tori peering out the window. After several minutes of uncomfortable conversation between the four of them, Clara made an excuse about needing to get back to town, and Colt walked her out. No doubt so they could talk without prying eyes and ears.

As far as Logan was concerned, whatever Colt and Clara had together wasn't anyone's business. They were two consenting adults who'd made no promises to each other. That wasn't a bad arrangement if both people agreed.

Suddenly memories from last night came flooding back, memories he knew wouldn't fade for a long time. The feel of Tori's flesh under his hand, or those soft gasps she'd made when he touched her. He closed his eyes, reliving the incredible feeling when his body joined with hers.

His blood stirred and he shifted in his chair. Even if he wanted a relationship, he knew there were too many obstacles stood in their way.

Tori brushed her glossy black hair off her shoulders and glanced at him. "I think Clara is trying not to cry. I feel so bad."

"Why, Tori? You had nothing to do with this. It's between your dad and Clara. They're both adults."

She came to the table. Her midnight gaze met his. "Sometimes, that doesn't stop someone from getting hurt. It's obvious Clara has feelings for my father. He had to know that. Yet nothing seems to matter except his precious Lucia."

"Clara knew Colt's heart belonged to someone else."

"And that's supposed to make it okay? What if she didn't plan for it to happen? I mean... look at me. I've regretted so many things from my past, which I can't seem to get away from." Once again, she turned those dark eyes on him. She was so beautiful it made him ache.

She sighed. "Knowing what I know now, I've discovered I was never in love with Dane. How can you love someone you don't respect? But by the time I realized that, I was in too deep. Maybe that was because my father wasn't ever around to guide me about men, to give me love and support."

Logan hated seeing her pain. "He's here now, Tori."

"Well, now's too late."

He shook his head. "No, Tori, it isn't too late. He's right outside, and you can start building a relationship now. I know because ten years ago, I walked away from my grandfather."

Revealing his past might be hard but he wanted to. After rising from the table, he began pacing. "I was angry and thought I knew it all. I said some pretty awful things to him." He paused, still hearing the cruel accusations in his head. "We hadn't talked in years, then the day I got shot… I laid there in that alley thinking about Nate and all I put him through. How badly I wanted to take back every bad thing, but then I lost consciousness, thinking I would die without telling Nate how sorry I was… for everything. Then by some miracle I lived through it. When I opened my eyes days later, my grandfather was standing beside my hospital bed."

Swallowing hard, he looked at Tori and saw the tears on her face. He went to her, but couldn't touch her, or he'd be lost. "Aw, Tori, don't cry. Just know that life is fleeting, and you never know how much time we have left. Colt has been trying to make an effort to patch up the past. I'm not saying you have to run into his arms. Just give him a chance."

She wiped her fingers across her cheeks, removing traces of tears. "And what if he turns his back on me again?" She shook her head. "Just like with Clara?"

"His...romantic relationships have nothing to do with you or your sisters."

Her dark gaze met his. "Don't you see a pattern here? Colt doesn't want any attachments. Maybe it's just with women. Do you think if we'd been sons, he'd feel this way?"

Why am I even involved in this discussion? "He let Clara know that he didn't want a serious relationship."

She froze then her chin jutted up. "That's it? Just explain the rules of the game so no one gets hurt. Is that what you did last night, Logan? Explained the rules to me so I won't get my hopes up for anything more?"

He released a long breath, hating that this petite woman could push his buttons. He never should have let her get so close because when she learned the truth... "I don't know the rules myself, but I don't think I can be what you want."

She walked up to him and stood as close as possible. "You have no idea what I want or need, Logan, so stop saying that."

Just then the door opened and Colt walked in. He didn't look too good, either.

Tori turned and glared. "I hope Clara ripped off a piece of your hide."

Colt straightened at his daughter's anger. "She got a pretty good chunk. You want some, too?"

Tori looked at Logan, then back at her father. She shook her head. "It's not worth my time. But

I'm not leaving Colton Creek without a fight. I'm renting the bunkhouse to anglers and running cattle."

Colt spoke up. "I'm not here to make you go home, Tori. I'm worried about you."

"Well, stop it, both of you. I've managed to take care of myself for the past ten years." She turned and walked upstairs to her bedroom.

Colt turned to Logan. "I know why she's angry with me, but what did you do?"

***

Hours later, Tori was still thinking about what a fool she'd been. Why was she so lousy when it came to choosing men? She hadn't been able to pick her father, but Logan...

Even with his warning about her not getting involved with him, she'd already fallen in love with the man. Once again, she needed to pick up the pieces and make it on her own. And she wanted a life here on the Colton Creek Ranch.

Unable to hold out any longer in her bedroom, she headed downstairs to use the facilities. She glanced at the clock. The time was nearly ten. She walked down the stairs and into the dark living area. Only the light over the stove spotlighted her path.

After making a trip to the bathroom, she came out and looked at the closed bedroom door. She leaned against the door to hear the sound of snoring. Logan?

"I wouldn't wake Colt if I were you."

She gasped and swung around to find Logan sitting on the sofa. She walked toward him and saw he'd didn't have on a shirt, only a pair of jeans. There was a wadded up blanket beside him. "What are you doing sleeping here?"

"Your father is in the bed. I offered to sleep here."

She shook her head. "Why aren't you in your apartment?"

"I can't protect you from there." He held out a hand. "We need to talk, Tori."

No matter how much she wanted to curl up next to him, she couldn't get close again. She'd already made a fool of herself last night. "We already said as much as needs to be said, Logan."

"Then listen to what I have to say." He continued to offer his hand.

She refused it, but sat on the coffee table across from him. "Okay, I'm listening."

His shadowed gaze met hers. "I never intended to hurt you." He glanced away as if trying to find a way to ease her down gently.

"You don't owe me any explanation, Logan. I came to you last night. I knew you didn't want any attachments. I don't expect any."

"God, woman, you don't get it at all. You came barreling in here, I wasn't expecting... any of this to happen." He waved a hand in the air. "Dammit, I want you more than any other woman I've ever met. Making love to you was incredible."

With a trembling hand, she reached out and touched his face. "You act as if it's a bad thing."

Logan covered her hand with his, then turned his head and kissed her palm. He watched her shiver.

"It wasn't that," he began. "I had my life all planned out. Nate and I were going to run cattle here. All the bad stuff I'd gone through would be left in the past. Then Nate died, and you showed up..."

"Sorry," she whispered. "Did I mess up your plans?"

She had no idea. "You sure as hell complicated them."

"You mean like this." She leaned forward and covered his mouth with hers then placed her hands on his chest.

He felt her cool fingers against his heated skin.

Need and want shot through Logan. He couldn't stop himself and he wrapped his arms around her and pulled her onto his lap. He took the chaste kiss deeper, but he still couldn't get enough of her.

He worshiped her with his mouth, with his hands as they slipped under her shirt and cupped her perfect breasts. He pinched the nipples and loved her soft whimper.

She broke off the kiss and arched against his body. "Oh, Logan. Please, I want you."

He nearly gave in. "With your father sleeping behind that door?"

Her breath tickled his earlobe. "We could go upstairs to my room."

He couldn't tell her how tempted he was, especially when an ache spread through him that had everything to do with his intense need for this woman. Yet, he couldn't keep going on until she knew the truth.

"No, I can't do this, Tori." He sat her upright and held her at arms' length. "I need to tell you something."

"Okay..."

He placed his elbows on his knees and thought a moment. "You know that I've been working to enlarge our herd." With her nod, he went on. "We'd planned to lease BLM land."

"That's a good idea."

Logan hesitated, and then finally said, "I've put in a conflicting bid on the Colton Creek's lease land."

At first, Tori looked confused, and then it slowly began to sink in. To mask her pain, she looked away, but he saw it.

"How long ago?"

"I put in the bid months ago, long before you came here. For the past year, Nate tried to find out what Colt was doing with the ranch, but your father never would give him a straight answer. Come on, Tori. Your father had lost interest in Colton Creek altogether."

Tori stood, trying to take it all in, but the hurt and anger got in the way. "I've been here a month and you never found a chance to tell me?"

With a strong push, Logan stood, too. She couldn't help but be distracted by his bare chest, then her gaze lowered to his unbuttoned Levis and she remembered last night with him. Now she knew what mistake their lovemaking had been.

"At first..."

Logan's voice drew her attention back to his face. "I wasn't sure if you were really staying, then when you talked about wanting to run a herd..."

Tori suddenly spoke up. "And then I complicated things and slept with you. Then Colt showed up."

"Yeah, that about sums it up," he told her.

Her hurt felt like betrayal, crushing her, making it hard to breath. She once again had let a man cloud her judgment.

Why would she think Logan could be different?

CHAPTER TWELVE

The next morning, Logan climbed off the sofa before dawn. He hadn't gotten much sleep, so he might as well get some work done. Anyway, he didn't think Tori wanted him hanging around the cabin.

He should be glad she'd stopped seeing him as some sort of good guy. He'd seen the dark side of life, and just wanted to come back here to start over. He was also the man who was trying to take her grazing land.

He made coffee, and once it was brewed, he poured some in his cup, and then allowed himself a few minutes to drink it. Leaving the cup in the sink, he started for the door when he heard Colt call out.

"If you wait up a minute, I'll give you a hand with the chores."

Logan hesitated, but how could he say no? "Not a problem. I'll have another cup then."

Already dressed, Colt went into the bathroom and returned a short time later. "Is Tori still asleep?"

Logan shrugged. "I haven't heard a sound from upstairs."

Colt took a drink from the mug, Logan handed him. "Look, Logan. I need to apologize for barging in yesterday. I should have let Tori and you know I was coming here. The truth is, I was afraid my daughter would make excuses not to see me. I'd let things drift between us after she came back from LA."

Logan didn't want to get involved in family matters, but in reality he already was. "This is your ranch, Colt. You have every right to come here."

Colt's fatigue appeared around his eyes, showing all his fifty-plus years. "I haven't always done right by my daughters. Not for a long time." His gaze met Logan's head on. "For that I'm ashamed and I plan to change that if I can. If Tori will let me."

"Going to take time."

Colt nodded. He hoped to God that time would heal the family. "If Tori's attitude last night is any indication, you're probably right. Did you get a chance to talk with her?"

Logan shrugged. "I won't be much help to you. I told her about my conflicting bid on the lease, and she didn't take the news well."

Colt sighed. Great, he'd forgotten about that issue. He'd let so much go with this ranch over the last few years. "Seems we're both in the dog house." He shook his head. "Never thought I'd see Tori be so assertive. She has always been so shy, letting her twin sister do all the talking. Maybe Tori's coming here has been good for her."

"Except Buckley has found her now."

He had no doubt Logan would watch out of Tori. "We need to catch the bastard," Colt said. "I know you were in law enforcement, you got any ideas on how to get this crazy?"

"Unless Buckley makes a mistake, we'll never get evidence to convict him." He looked Colt in the eye. "The only other way is to have Tori contact him and bring him out in the open. In other words, use her as bait."

***

By midmorning, Tori was going stir crazy inside the cabin. The only good thing about the situation was she hadn't had to face her father, or Logan. They'd been gone before she got up.

She definitely didn't want to talk to either of them, especially Logan. She'd already made a fool of herself. Not saying she hadn't been warned, but over a man who only wanted her land was humiliating.

Well, she was done hiding out. She grabbed her hat off the hook, walked out the cabin door and into the bright sunlight. With determined strides she headed across the compound toward the barn and caught sight of the painters' truck parked at the bunkhouse. *Good.* At least she could move ahead with something. She needed to let Clara know the place would be ready to rent out by next weekend.

With new determination, she picked up her pace. If her father wanted her to leave, then he would have to throw her off the property.

No one would keep her from starting her new life. She didn't need to partner with Logan McNeely, either. And she wasn't about to give up the grazing lease without a fight. She'd talk to her father and offer to pay it herself. She had money saved. Then she'd hire help and run her own herd. She could supplement the cost with income from her design business.

She refused to let another man control her happiness, or her future. She'd run the Colton Creek and Logan could run the Double M. They'd be neighbors, but never, never lovers again.

She walked into the cool barn, happy to see she was alone except for the horses. Heading down the center aisle she greeted Ace, Buffy and Smoky, and then she saw Domino.

Hearing her voice, he'd come to the gate. He blew air out of his nostrils in greeting.

"Hey, fella. How are you doing today?" She would miss this guy if he went back with Logan to his ranch.

Domino pressed his head against her body, begging for more attention.

"Sorry, I haven't been to see you lately." She buried her face against his soft muzzle, and felt her stress easing away. She didn't want to think any more. Not about her father, her mother, not Logan.

"How about we break out of this jail?"

Domino made a neighing sound, and danced around the stall, letting her know his excitement.

She smiled. "Okay, okay, but we can't let anyone know."

With a final pat, she went off to the tack room and ten minutes later she had a saddle on Domino. After a minor adjustment to the stirrups, she stepped back to allow the animal to get used to the added weight. She'd seen such a big improvement in the once-abused gelding over the past month. Last week she'd ridden him bareback. Now, she hoped to see if he would take a saddle and her.

"Come on, boy. We're going for a ride." She walked him out of the barn, but came around the opposite side to the far gate, staying clear of the bunkhouse where she suspected Colt and Logan were.

Once outside the corral, she stuck her booted foot into the stirrup and swung her leg over Domino's back. She picked up the reins and the horse danced sideways.

"Whoa, fella." She kept her voice soft and calm. Finally, Domino settled down and she started the animal toward the meadow. And freedom for them both.

She began in a walk, then she nudged him into a two-beat trot. She loved how he responded to her commands. "Good boy," she praised. "Okay, I think you're ready to go."

Tori pushed down her hat to secure it on her head, then dug her heels into his sides and the horse took off. No coaxing was involved, Domino knew what to do. She leaned low in the saddle, let the gelding take the lead and quickly discovered he loved to run.

So did she. Feeling the wind against her face was good as they raced across the open pasture toward the mountain range. So much time had passed since she felt this type of freedom, from everything and everybody.

Fifteen minutes later, horse and rider arrived at the creek that ran through the center of the ranch. Tori pulled back on the reins and slowed the animal, then finally they stopped at the edge of the rocky bank. She climbed down and felt her legs go weak for a moment. She hadn't ridden that hard in a long time.

"We need to do this more often," she told the horse as she checked him. She ran a hand over his scarred hindquarters. He seemed fine, in fact better than fine. She walked him to the water's edge, allowing him to drink. She too, crouched down and drank from the clear cold water.

Once she'd quenched her thirst, she looked around the grove of trees that shaded the bank. She couldn't help but remember the last time she'd ridden here with Logan to check the cattle herd and they spied the herd of mustangs. The spot where they'd shared lunch wasn't far from here.

She closed her eyes, recalling how they'd nearly made love that afternoon. Until he put a stop to their actions. What a fool she'd been to keep pursuing him. He didn't want anything permanent, not with her anyway.

Sad, she sat on a fallen log, wishing she could erase the past few days. At least, she'd have her pride left. Problem was, she was still in love with him.

Domino shifted and whinnied, letting her know something or someone was close by. She stood ready to get on her horse, praying that Dane hadn't found her out here. Oh, God. Had she put everyone in danger? Then she felt relieved when she recognized Smoky and Colt's trademark hat, a dung-colored Stetson.

In an unhurried stride, her father walked the dapple gray mustang toward the water, and then climbed down, letting the horse drink.

"What are you doing out here?" she asked, though she already knew the answer.

"We got worried when we saw you ride off alone so we flipped a coin. I won."

Was he talking about Logan, too?

He came toward her. "Until Dane is found, you're not safe. I know you're angry with Logan and me, but you can't just take off and not tell anyone."

"Now I'm being held prisoner?"

With a shake of his head, he sighed. "Come on, Tori. We're trying to protect you."

"I'm fine. I've been on my own since college. So you can go back to Montana." She walked back to her log and sat, knowing she didn't mean what she said. Despite her trumped-up bravado, she knew her father was right. She hadn't protected herself from Dane.

Her father eased down beside her. "I deserve your fury, Tori, but I want to help you."

"No one can help me." Sadness washed over her. Her life was so messed up. "Dane will never let me go." She looked at him. He was different than the man who raised her, not just his age, but his demeanor. Could he have changed? "I won't come back to Montana because he'll only follow me there."

"Then we'll fight him together." He huffed out a breath. "Dammit, Tori, I can't sit back and not do anything. You're my daughter and I love you."

She felt tears well in her eyes. She couldn't ever remember hearing those words from him. Suddenly, she couldn't stop the rush of tears as a sob tore from her throat.

"Oh, sweetheart." Colt put his arms around her and he gathered her close. "I'm so sorry. So sorry, I haven't been there for you, for all you girls." He rubbed her back in a circling motion, and she never wanted to leave the safety of his protection.

"I can't change those years, but please, let me help you now."

She finally pulled herself together and raised her head. "I don't want to leave here." She glanced at him. "I know it's crazy, but I've found a connection with Rachel. I can run this place. Clara has assured me I can make money from renting space to anglers.

With the extra money I can increase the herd, and hire ranch hands."

Colt shook his head. "We're losing the lease on part of the grazing land. There isn't enough money to reinvest. It's my fault for not keeping a closer eye on the finances."

"You can't help that you were ill," she said as her chest tightened, realizing how close they'd come to losing him. "Are you sure you're okay now?"

He smiled, and the lines around his eyes deepened. "I'm what the doctors are calling a miracle. I have few leftover effects from the stroke. My smile is a little crooked, but at least I'm smiling now. My left arm still has some weakness, but I'm continuing to do physical therapy."

"I'm just glad you're better. I watched you ride up. I was impressed by how good you look."

"Well, your older sister, Ana, was relentless about me getting better."

Tori knew their mother reappearing was another incentive. "And Lucia. Her coming back might be another reason, too."

Colt studied her. "We don't need to talk about her, I know the subject upsets you."

"But you're happy she's returned."

For a long time, he looked toward the water, then finally said, "It's true, I never stopped loving your mother. But as you know first-hand, obsessing about her wasn't healthy for me." He paused. "I still have resentment that she left us. So many of the details of her story are hard to believe. The private investigator researched her husband, Vicente Santoya. He's well known in Mexico as one of the biggest, most ruthless drug dealers. Your mother's father, Cesar Delgado, was tied in with them."

"I still can't understand why she could never contact us."

His blued-eyed gaze turned to her. "She was pregnant when she was taken back to Mexico. If Santoya had found out..." He shook his head. "I don't want to think about what he would have done. I want the chance to get to know my twin sons, Quintin and Rafael."

Tori felt the familiar pang of rejection. "You always wanted sons."

Colt reached out and took hold of her hands. "I've never given you any reason to trust me and I'll never make father of the year, but I've always loved you girls. Quinn and Rafe are my flesh and blood, too. So I'm asking for a second chance to be your father, as well as theirs."

All her life, Tori had wished for this moment. "You don't have to do anything, just love us."

He hugged her close. "Oh, baby girl, I will until I take my last breath."

She buried her face in his big burly chest as so many emotions washed over her. A knot deep inside loosened as she spoke, "I love you, too, Dad."

Colt raised his head. He was unashamed of his tears. All he cared about was his daughter's love. "Those are the best words I could ever hear." He leaned forward and kissed her cheek.

"Now, how can I help you with this Buckley guy? Besides string him up to the nearest tree."

"I just want him to go away," she said, leaning her head on his shoulder.

Colt grew serious. He would make sure they found this bastard. "Then you need to let Logan help you."

In a quick move, she stood and walked toward the horses. She felt her father behind her.

"You want to talk about it?" he asked, hoping he had some good advice.

She shrugged. "Same old story, I picked the wrong guy... again."

"If your old man's opinion means anything, I don't think you picked the wrong guy. I think Logan is still handling some ghosts from his past. I've known him since he came to live with Nate." Colt smiled, remember the skinny kid with a bad attitude. Nate had been so proud when he graduated college and got a job in law enforcement.

"That kid had a major chip on his shoulder. He outgrew that when he joined the police force. Nate was so proud of him."

"Logan misses him."

"So do I." All those years he'd come here and talk with Nate, and share problems. "There wasn't a better man, a helluva horseman, too. Logan is doing a fine job with the ranch. I like his idea about running an organic herd." Colt looked at her. "Give Logan some time. He's had a major loss in his life."

"Logan doesn't want me in his life."

Colt arched an eyebrow. Something told him Logan cared more than even he knew. "Are we talking about the man who has ignored his own ranch because he's been stuck to your side protecting you?" His smile turned into a big grin. "Logan's problem is he wants you so much, he can't walk away."

***

Logan leaned against the corral fence watching Colt and Tori ride in. He felt a sense of relief as the two climbed down from their mounts. He caught Tori's smiling at her father and his chest constricted, wishing she would direct one at him.

Colt spoke first. "Thank you, Logan, for letting me borrow Smoky. As soon as I take care of the horses, I'm packing up and heading home. You two can handle things here." He started off toward the barn.

Logan stopped him. "I'll do it. I need to check out Domino anyway."

Colt hesitated, but then handed over his reins and walked toward the house. He held out his hand to Tori.

She didn't relinquish her reins. "I rode him, I'll brush him down."

Logan wasn't happy she'd taken off with the gelding, but when he saw those dark eyes were red from tears, he decided a lecture could wait. "How'd he do with the saddle?"

"A little skittish at first, then no problems at all."

They walked inside the barn and Logan directed her toward the bathing section. He removed the tack from Smoky as Tori worked next to him in silence. That was one of the things he liked about her, she didn't feel the need to fill up the silence with meaningless conversation.

Twenty minutes later both horses had been groomed and placed back into their clean stalls. Tori started out of the barn, leaving him behind. No way was she getting away this time. He reached for her arm and turned her to face him.

"We need to talk, Tori."

"I think everything has been said. Maybe you should just pack up and go back to your ranch."

"And you're staying here alone?"

"I have my twenty-two. If Dane shows up I'll shoot him and put an end to my problem."

"Yeah, like he'll walk in the front door and announce himself." Rather than heading toward another argument, he released a long breath. "Why don't you go back to Montana with Colt?" God, he didn't want her to leave, but he couldn't ask her to stay. He couldn't admit how much she'd come to mean to him. "Going will be the best thing."

"For you, or for me?" She stood her ground, hand planted on her hips. "I'm not leaving here, Logan. This is going to be my home. I'll hire help, but I will make a living here."

Great. "What about the partnership on the herd?"

"Do you think we can be partners? You weren't exactly honest about the land."

"If you remember, I did tell you. I just waited until you decided to stay here. I might be a lot of things Tori, but I'm not so low as to try and steal your land. If you want to ranch, by all means, have at it."

He saw her surprised look, and then she quickly masked it. "Well... thank you. I mean what I said; I don't want you staying in the cabin. I have security cameras and an alarm system now."

Stubborn woman. "Okay, you're the boss. I'll move my things back to the apartment by tonight."

She opened her mouth to argue, but shut it. "Thank you for all your help." She turned and walked away, leaving him to ponder what he was losing. Yet, he couldn't go after her.

***

Hours had gone by since Colt left and reluctantly started back to Montana. Before the man climbed in his truck, Logan promised he'd take care of Tori.

As promised, Logan had moved his things out of the cabin. Yet, he hadn't taken his eyes off the security camera's pictures on his computer screen in the apartment.

Tori could be stubborn, but he would protect her. Cameras had been installed at the front door, the back door and surrounding windows.

And he would get this guy.

As he sat at the desk, Logan took a bite of ham sandwich and a drink of his iced tea. He'd much rather be eating some of Tori's stew, or pot roast. Then afterward he'd head off to bed with her.

Memories from two nights ago flashed in his head. He couldn't erase the picture of her walking into his room, coming into his bed. He wanted to resist her, but there was no way in hell he could.

He'd been unprepared by the fierceness of her desire. What man could turn that down? Or the taste of her mouth, or the feel of his hands on her body, that soft, sinuous body. The sensation of her moving against him, stroking him in all the right places, driving him over the edge... He gasped and opened his eyes.

He had to stop this craziness. Tori needed to go back to her family, and he needed to concentrate on his life here. Not on what he couldn't have, no matter how badly he wanted it. He'd let too many people get close only to lose them. He was better off not to risk his heart again.

All his attention went back to the computer screen and security camera. Something was wrong. The one at the back door to the cabin was out. Or someone had put it out.

Damn. He stood, grabbed his gun, and flashlight off the counter and rushed out the door. That jerk wasn't getting her, not if he had anything to do about it. He took off down the steps and hit the ground running.

He reached the cabin in record time and checked the front door. It looked fine, but he wasn't satisfied. Gun drawn, he pressed his body against the house and made his way around to the side, hearing an animal howling off in the distance, but everything else seemed quiet. He worked to slow his breathing as he reached the back of the cabin and found the door partly open.

His heart pounding, he knew something was wrong. Hesitantly, he pushed open the door and glanced into the darkness. He listened, but there wasn't a sound. Tightening his grip on his gun, he crossed the main room lit only by moonlight coming through the windows.

He quickly did his check of the main area, and then cautiously took the steps up to the second floor. He peered into Tori's bedroom. Her bed was messed up, but she wasn't in it. If Buckley had her, he couldn't have gotten very far. Maybe a five-minutes head start.

He glanced in the other bedroom upstairs then returned to Tori's to look for any clues left behind. That was when he heard a woman cry out and he glanced out the window. He saw two shadowy figures cutting across the field toward the road. Pulse racing, he pulled out his cell phone to call for backup.

No way in hell was Buckley taking Tori from him.

CHAPTER THIRTEEN

Tori fought the tight ropes around her wrists, refusing to go with Dane easily. Although he'd already hit her several times, she wasn't making the abduction easy. This time, she'd stand up to him, then she saw the gun. If they stayed in the cabin, she was worried Dane would shoot Logan. She couldn't let him get hurt because of her. And she knew he would come after her to save her. Tears blurred her eyes, at the fear she might never see him again.

"Stop stalling," Dane growled, giving her tied hands a hard tug. "No one is coming to rescue you, bitch. I made sure of that."

A chill ran through her. "What did you do? I swear if you hurt anyone, I will..."

He stopped and she stumbled against his body. "You'll what? You'll do nothing, because I'm in charge now." He smirked, his lips twisting into an ugly grimace. "That's been your problem,

Vicki; you've never learned who the boss is. Now, you're going to do everything I say." He twisted her arm and she winced. "Right?"

"Yes." Pain shot through her arm up to her shoulder. Memories of previous times he'd hurt her flooded her mind. "Please, stop."

At his release, she fell in the high grass, feeling the moisture seep through her pajama bottoms.

"Just remember that."

She studied the once handsome man. She hadn't seen him in a long time, nearly a year. He'd put on weight and his once-perfect blond hair was shaggy and dirty. He hadn't shaved in days. But it was the cold rage in his eyes that terrified her.

He gripped her arm again and pulled her up. "Come on, we need to get to the car and out of here."

No way could she get into a car with him. She saw the violent look in his eyes and she knew this time she wasn't sure if she'd survive.

"Please, Dane. Please release me before you get into more trouble. The police know it was you who broke into the cabin. I have a restraining order."

He ignored her as they came to a group of trees along the dirt road. She had on tennis shoes, but they weren't much protection against the rocky terrain. In the dark, she kept stumbling. Please, Logan, find me, she prayed silently. "Where are you taking me?"

"Wouldn't you like to know?"

He pulled her close, his head lowered. She smelled his rancid breath, his foul body odor. She struggled to keep from gagging.

"If you think that new boyfriend of yours will find you, forget it." He gave her another hard yank. "Now, come on."

Dane kept pulling at her, practically dragging her toward a car parked off the road. They were about a hundred yards from it when headlights appeared. He pushed her down behind a tree. Her heart raced with excitement on seeing the sheriff's patrol car race by, then suddenly screech to a halt. Hope sprang in her chest as two men got out of their vehicle, and with guns drawn, slowly approached the SUV.

Silently, Dane pulled her backward until they were far enough away that they couldn't be seen. She started to scream, but felt the cold barrel of his gun poking against her back.

"Please, Dane," she pleaded. "Let me go and you can escape faster."

With his free hand, he rubbed his temple. "Just shut up." He pulled her in another direction, farther away from the cabin.

Twenty minutes later, with the moonlight helping them find their way, they walked toward the vast mountain range and a group of rocks. Dane took out his flashlight searching the rock face for something, and then they came to an opening.

Once inside, he pushed her down to the damp ground, then he turned on a battery powered lantern, adding a slow glow to the small, dirty space. After her eyes adjusted to the light, she glanced around to find a sleeping bag and some camping gear. How long had Dane been here, watching her? Logan. Would he ever be able to find her?

"You try to run off, I'll tie your feet," he threatened with an angry gaze. Then he grinned. "I want to save that until later when I have you all to myself. First, we're getting out of this Godforsaken place." He pulled out his cell phone. "Stay put."

He left her and stepped out of the cave, but stayed in the entrance, then after a few minutes, he returned. "Our ride will be here soon, and then you're mine for good."

***

While Sheriff Harris and his deputy combed the surrounding area of the abandoned vehicle, Logan headed to the barn. He would do his own search. After grabbing a saddle, he headed toward Ace when he was distracted by a ruckus in Domino's stall. The animal was kicking the boards as he cried out in a high-pitched whinny.

Logan went to the stall. "Hey, fella, calm down." He took hold of the halter and stroked his muzzle to calm the horse. "We're gonna find her." He didn't know how or why, but this animal had formed a special connection with Tori.

He attached a lead rope and walked the horse out of the stall, then grabbed the saddle and began to tack up the gelding.

Five minutes later, he led the animal outside, and made a call to Colt. He had to let him know he hadn't kept his daughter from Buckley. Logan jammed his cell phone back in his pocket and tucked his Glock into his holster, and then he swung a leg over Domino's back.

The moonlight would help the search, but there were other dangers in the night. A horse could stumble in the uneven terrain and they could both break their necks. Or meet up with wild animals that hunted their prey in the darkness.

Logan didn't care about any of that. His police instincts took over as he kicked his boots into the horse's sides and took off back toward the search party. He would find Tori. He had to, or he might not survive losing her.

He'd joined the group of the men combing the area around the vehicle. Logan rode farther out through a group of trees. Using his flashlight, he climbed off Domino and together they walked around. He saw a spot where the long grass had been trampled down as if someone had been lying here. Was it an animal or a person?

With the light as his guide, he continued on the path, seeing a trail of flattened grass. In the dirt, he saw two sets of footprints, large ones and smaller ones.

He called over to the sheriff and pointed to the discovery. "We're seeing something similar over the other side of the vehicle heading toward town."

Logan looked toward the mountains. He wasn't sure which direction to go. "Makes sense that they would head to town," he said. "Buckley could steal a car and get out of the area."

Suddenly, Harris's cell phone rang and he answered right away. "Harris, here," he said, then listened to the caller. "It's Detective Brandon from LA," he told Logan, then spoke into the phone. "Could I talk to Buckley's father?" the sheriff asked the detective, then walked away for few minutes. Logan tensed, wanting to know what Buckley's daddy had to do with this situation.

"That was Dane Buckley's father. Seems he finally believes his son has a problem and contacted the LA police. Dane called him about thirty minutes ago and asked for a helicopter to come pick him up."

For the first time in over an hours, Logan felt a sense of hope. "Did he say where his son was?"

"Outside of Dawson Springs... in a cave."

"Cave?" Logan tried to think of any caves in the area. "He's got Tori holed up in a cave?"

Tom Harris nodded. "You've lived out here since you were a kid, McNeely, you know of any caves?"

"Man, it's been a long time since I've climbed around on the rocks. There's probably some hole somewhere, maybe enough space and cover to protect you from the elements." Logan swung back into the saddle.

The sheriff held up a hand. "Hey, hold up for a deputy to go with you."

Logan whirled the horse around. "You better deputize me because I'm going after him."

"All right, consider yourself deputized, but dammit, Logan, Buckley is dangerous."

"Don't you think I know that? But he's got Tori. There's no time." Digging in his heels, he took off toward the foothills, not wanting to think what the creep was doing to her. Buckley wasn't getting away this time, not if he had to track him all over the county.

Logan rode as fast as was safe toward the huge rock formation. Once there, he climbed down and had to find the rest of the way in the dark. Doing his best to keep calm, he walked around the boulder, looking for any way in. It couldn't be too difficult. He doubted Buckley had any wilderness training, but that didn't mean he couldn't pull off this abduction.

He looked for anything that would help find them. Then he saw a flash of white on the ground. The belt to Tori's robe.

He looked for more footprints but soon the ground became too rocky to track. He left Domino tied to a tree, knowing he couldn't handle the terrain anyway. Careful not to set pebbles loose, he climbed up, but hadn't made much progress until he saw a dim light coming from behind a large boulder.

Pressed flat against the rock, Logan moved slowly toward the light, and then he heard a man's voice. He peered around the edge and saw Buckley pacing, holding his cell phone against his ear.

The man wore jeans and a dirty shirt and it must have been days since he'd bathed. His hair and beard looked just as bad. The one thing that really worried him was the gun he saw stuck into Buckley's waistband.

"You promised to help me, Dad," Buckley argued into the phone. "Don't lie to me."

Logan looked further inside the rock overhang to see Tori curled up on the floor. She looked tired and dirty, but otherwise she appeared unhurt for now. He felt relief loosen the knot of panic in his gut, but he glanced back at the agitated Buckley, and knew he had to get her out of there and soon.

Tori wanted to cry. Nothing she'd said to Dane would change the situation. He wasn't ever letting her go. And now he was so angry with his father she knew she'd pay the price.

So if she wanted out of this mess, it was her job to get away. She couldn't keep expecting people to rescue her.

She looked down at her tied hands. Her wrists were raw, but she'd managed to loosen the knots, soon she'd have them off. When she looked around for some sort of weapon to defend herself, she caught some movement outside. She squinted, her breath caught in her throat. Oh, God. It was Logan. He'd come for her. She glanced at Dane on the phone.

"I told you, I need you to get me out of here. You promised, Dad. You said they couldn't hurt me and you wouldn't let me go to jail."

Dane listened awhile. "No, I'm not going to any hospital. I need to be with Vicki. We're in love. We just need to go away and we'll be happy. So you send me that helicopter." He hung up and threw the phone on the ground. "He's not coming, but I don't need him." He stomped close, grabbed her by the arm and pulled her to her feet. "Let's go."

She resisted, leaning against his grasp. "Where?"

"I told you to stop asking me so many questions." He frowned. "I have a headache."

"Dane, I'm trying to help. We can't leave unless we know where we're going."

He paused and studied her suspiciously. "Why are you being so cooperative suddenly?"

Keeping her gaze averted, she shrugged. "You like me better playing hard to get?" She was winging it. "Am I just fun when you're stalking me, or breaking into my apartment and destroying my things?"

He grinned. "That was your fault. You needed to be taught a lesson. And getting Josie was even better. She never liked me. She's the one who convinced you to break it off with me."

Tori wasn't about to argue.

"You all were so stupid, including that hot shot Detective Brandon. He couldn't pin anything on me. I was too smart to leave any clues or fingerprints."

Suddenly, fury flashed in Dane's eyes. "But then you came here and slept with another man." His fist clenched tight.

She tried not to react to what was coming. "You're mine, Vicki, and no one else's. Do I have to convince you?" When he raised his fist, she braced for the first blow, but it never came.

Instead, she opened her eyes to see Logan tackling Dane. As the two rolled around on the floor, she scrambled away. She tugged at her restraints and finally broke loose. She grabbed a stick from the wood pile as Dane cursed and managed to pull his gun. She screamed a warning, and Logan knocked the weapon away just as he fired. When it fell to the ground, she grabbed it as the fighting men rolled close. Then the sheriff and two deputies rushed in.

Tom Harris pulled Logan off Dane. Dane began whining about police brutality as he was handcuffed and led out. He paused at the door and looked at over his shoulder. "I love you, Vicki. You're mine."

"No, Dane." She shook her head. "I was never yours."

Logan went to her and pulled her into his arms. She felt herself trembling, but even held in Logan's embrace, she couldn't stop.

He pulled back and searched her face. "Are you all right?" he asked as he checked the marks on her wrists.

She nodded at the strong man before her. Thank God, he wasn't hurt.

Logan reached out and touched her face. "I hate that he put his hands on you, Tori. But he's never coming near you again."

Her emotions were close to spilling out. She couldn't do that in front of him. "I'm okay now. Thank you, Logan."

He didn't look convinced. "I need to take you to the emergency room."

"No, I'm fine. I want to go home, back to the cabin."

The sheriff had other ideas. She answered some basic questions, and then Logan informed everyone he'd bring her into town to give her statement tomorrow.

Without waiting for a response, he helped Tori out of the cave and down the slope. Once on solid ground, she drew in a huge gulp of air that helped ease her trembling.

That was when she heard the familiar whinny and then she saw Domino. She didn't know where she got the strength but she rushed to him and wrapped her arms around his neck.

"Oh, Domino," she cried. "How's my guy?" She rubbed his sides and hugged his neck, letting the tears finally fall. The nightmare was over. She looked at Logan coming toward her.

So were her dreams.

***

The trip took nearly thirty minutes, but Logan got Tori back to the cabin. He'd called Colt and let him know what had happened, then he handed the phone to Tori while he got Domino settled back in his stall.

"Is Colt coming back?"

"I convinced him to stay in a hotel tonight and come back in the morning, that he can meet me at the sheriff's office."

"Good, you need to rest."

He turned off the lights in the barn and walked Tori up to the cabin, his arm around her waist to steady her. She was exhausted and looked so fragile, but was stubborn about asking for his help. He offered to call Clara to come out. When she refused to disturb her friend, he sent her off to take a shower. He camped outside the door, and his heart nearly broke when he heard her ragged sobs. Then she finally emerged from the bathroom. He poured her a cup of tea. He'd never felt so helpless in his life.

"I thought this might help you sleep."

She shook her head, and tucked a wet strand of hair behind an ear. "I don't want to sleep." She shivered and leaned against the counter. "I've never seen Dane like this before."

"He's probably been sick a long time," Logan told her. As a former cop, he knew this situation could have turned out much differently. "His father just kept covering for him, and never paid attention to his son's real problem."

Logan looked at her freshly scrubbed face and damp hair, hanging around her shoulders, her eyes sad, and her lips slightly swollen. He broke his promise to himself and reached out and touched the faint bruise on her jaw.

"Oh, God, Tori, I could kill him for hurting you."

She pulled away. "No, he's not worth it." She rubbed her hands over her arms. "Look, Logan, you don't have to stay with me. With Dane in custody, I'm no longer in danger."

God, how could he leave her? He'd nearly lost her tonight. "I'm not going anywhere, Tori. And I don't think you want to be alone, either."

Her dark gaze met his, and he lost all his willpower. He reached for her and drew her into his arms. "Oh, God, babe. I was so scared when I couldn't get to you. If anything had happened to you, I don't know what I would have done."

In the circle of his embrace, he felt her small body trembling. He tightened his hold trying to absorb her fears, her sadness.

He placed kisses along her forehead, then moved down to her cheek, and then either side of her mouth.

Then he finally captured her mouth fiercely, like a man who'd been starved and suddenly found a banquet. He was hungry... for her.

Tori knew this was wrong, but she couldn't seem to stop. All she wanted to do was erase the last few hours, the pain and fear. She needed to feel Logan's strong arms clutching her tightly, his hard body pressed against hers. She savored the taste of his mouth on hers.

In frustration, she stood on tiptoe and tightened her arms around his neck, pressing her breasts against the hard muscles of his chest. She still wanted more contact, so she rubbed against him, causing her nipples to harden.

He broke off the kiss. "Tori, this isn't a good idea. You're in shock over what happened."

A shiver raced through her as she arched against him, pushing her hips closer. "I know what I'm doing, Logan. I want you to make love to me. I want you to wipe away all the ugliness from my mind."

He hesitated.

"I'm just a woman, Logan, who needs to be loved to feel whole again, even if that feeling is just for tonight."

He looked away, his expression as stony as the mountains he'd rescued her from. "If I kiss you again, I'm not stopping until I finish what you've started. I don't want you to have any regrets."

"Then kiss me, Logan," she insisted, then held her breath.

"Bossy, aren't you?"

He trapped her against the counter as their gazes locked.

On seeing the desire revealed in his eyes, she nearly moaned. "When I need to be."

Without saying another word, he reached down and lifted her into his arms, then carried her into the bedroom. He set her down beside the bed and began taking off her clothes, slowly. Once she was naked, he stood back, waiting.

With trembling fingers, she worked the buttons on his denim shirt, craving his skin against hers. Once she exposed more of the hard muscles beneath, she drew a breath.

Logan was rough and strong and male, she discovered as her fingertip traced his skin. She wanted to get drunk on this man. Her senses whirling she kissed him. When he nudged apart her lips, she welcomed him with a moan.

He made a low sound in his chest then pulled away, gasping for air. "I want you, Tori."

She looked up to see his desire, even if it was only for tonight. She wanted him, too. "Make me forget, Logan. Love me."

He took her mouth again, and lowered her to the bed, and he came down on top of her, covering her with his body...

***

Around four the next morning, Logan reluctantly left Tori asleep in bed. He wanted nothing more than to keep her wrapped in his arms, and not let anything happen to her ever again. Except life had taught him that safety nets didn't exist, people left him anyway, and Tori would do the same.

After scribbling a note, he went to go feed the stock. He finished in record time, then jumped in his truck and took the back road over to the Double M to check his own herd.

He did want to go with her into town to give her statement to the sheriff. He didn't want her to go through it alone. Then once the legal part with Buckley was finished, they had to move on. He needed to get used to the idea of not being a part of Tori's life.

His thoughts went back to what happened last night. He had been a fool to think making love to her would change anything. She was vulnerable and she needed him. He'd let down his guard, too, and somehow, she slipped right into his heart. Now the pain was worse because he had to let her go.

He pulled his truck up at the house and saw Seth Cameron coming down the road in his jeep.

He climbed out of the cab. "Hey, what are you doing here?"

"Trying to be a good neighbor and check on your herd," he answered with a wave toward the pasture.

"Thanks. I owe you one."

"I can't keep count of the times you've pulled me out of the gutter." Seth studied him. "How's Tori doing?"

Honestly, he wished he knew. "Not complaining about what she went through, but she had a rough time of it.

Sheriff wants her to go into town and give her statement. So I need to get back soon."

"She's lucky she has you around," his neighbor told him. "No telling what would have happened if you hadn't found her."

Pain tightened his throat. He didn't want to think about what Buckley was capable of. Tori was safe now, but she didn't need him any longer at the ranch, or in her life.

"You're thinking so hard, it's got to hurt."

He looked at Seth. "A lot has changed. Tori knows I tried to take over the lease."

"So give it back," Seth suggested. "You two were going to be partners anyway. My question is, will you make the partnership more permanent?"

"There won't be any partnership of any kind."

Seth frowned. "That's only because you're not willing to even give it a chance. Stubborn as hell, you are." He shook his head. "Women like Tori Slater don't get dropped in your lap everyday."

"I'm not looking for a relationship."

"Hell, what man is? Tell me this, can you live without her?" Seth raised a hand. "Remember, I live everyday wishing I could have more time with Ivy and my son. I know firsthand what hell it's like to be without someone you love." Pain was evident in his friend's eyes, and Logan had to look away. "Don't waste a minute of that precious time."

CHAPTER FOURTEEN

Colt had been waiting for her outside the sheriff's office when she'd driven into town. When her father opened his arms, she ran into them, accepting his comfort and support. She let go of more the tears. She thought she'd cried out last night. When she finally composed herself, she was ready to put Dane in jail.

Her nerves stretched thin, Tori glanced at the clock. She'd been here two hours and never expected the questions to be so grueling. Reliving every detail of Dane's abduction had been rough. She was glad she hadn't been alone.

Tom Harris stood from his desk chair. "Let me get this statement copied and then I'll just need your signature." The sheriff stepped out of his office.

She was left alone to think about Logan.

She could still feel his body pressed against hers during the night and then the coldness when he'd left the bed without any word. He'd made love to her so tenderly, so lovingly, she struggled not to love the man right back. Yet, he never spoke the words, and she doubted he ever would. That was why she wasn't ready to face Logan this morning. Since the day she'd arrived at the Colton Creek, she'd depended far too much on him.

And she had to stop.

Logan offered to drive her into town so she could give her statement, but she'd refused to let him. For her to repeat everything that Dane had done was far too humiliating. Her father waiting outside gave her enough reassurance.

The sheriff walked back inside with a copy of her statement. After she signed it, she would be able to leave. "What will happen to Dane? Will he be prosecuted for kidnapping me?"

"The DA thinks there's enough evidence for a conviction. Even if Buckley senior hires a hot shot criminal lawyer, and tries to get him extradited back to LA for a psychiatric evaluation, we'll fight it. We have hospitals in this state that can do it, and if I have to, I'll drive the guy to Cheyenne myself," he told her. "I also learned Detective Brandon got a search warrant for Buckley's apartment. They found numerous items that had been taken from your townhouse."

She didn't want anything that Dane touched. "So I need to go back to Los Angeles?"

He shook his head. "I believe with your testimony, we already have a solid case against him."

Tori nodded. "Good. I don't want Josie's life disturbed anymore." She glanced out though the glass partition and saw Logan talking with Colt. His gaze connected with hers and she felt that familiar stirring inside her. Maybe some time apart would change her feelings.

"Well, it looks like we're finished here."

"Thank you, sheriff." Tori stood and walked out toward the two men in the waiting area.

Colt hugged her. "How are you holding up?" he asked.

She shrugged. "I'm okay. Sheriff Harris has been very kind."

Logan spoke up. "The main thing is that Buckley isn't getting away with this again."

Just then, a tall distinguished-looking man came through the door. Although she'd never met Dane's father, Tori knew who he was since his son looked just like him. Her body stilled, and she grabbed her father's hand tight.

He crossed the room toward her. "Miss Slater," he called. "I'm Richard Buckley, and I wonder if I can have a moment of your time?"

The movement happened so fast it caught her off guard. Both Colt and Logan stepped in front of her, and Logan pushed the guy backward. "Miss Slater will do all her talking in court."

Mr. Buckley stood his ground. "I know what my son did was wrong."

"Then you shouldn't have kept getting him off," Logan said.

Buckley looked Logan up and down, and then he turned back to Tori. "I just wanted to say how sorry I am that I let it go this far. I know Dane needs help. I also will pay for any damages done to your townhouse in Los Angeles or here."

She stepped away from her father so the man could see her. "All I want, Mr. Buckley, is for Dane to get the help he needs, and to stay far away from me. I've had two years of looking over my shoulder and I refuse to be a prisoner any longer."

Mr. Buckley nodded. "I promise you, Miss Slater, there won't be anymore trouble from us."

No more. "That better be true because I refuse to give anyone any power over me again."

Richard Buckley nodded, then headed toward Sheriff Harris's office.

Suddenly feeling the walls closing in on her, Tori was unable to catch her breath. She had to get out of there. She rushed through the door and gasped some needed air into her lungs. She felt herself sway.

"You need to sit down." She heard Logan's voice and his hand on her back as he directed her to a bench on the sidewalk. "Put your head down."

She didn't have much choice. Embarrassed at her weakness, she did as he asked. After a few minutes, he let her up.

"Better?"

She couldn't look at him. "Yes. Thank you."

"You've gone through a lot in the last few days."

"It's over, sweetheart," Colt said and took her hand. "Try to put all of this out of your mind. Dane won't hurt you again."

She fought tears, feeling her throat close up. Please, she couldn't break down now. "I know."

"Have you eaten today?" Logan asked.

"I wasn't hungry."

Colt sent her an encouraging smile. "How about some lunch? My treat."

Tori shrugged. The last thing she wanted was food. "I'm not really hungry."

Logan stood. "Look, why don't you and your dad go and have lunch? I need to get back to the ranch, anyway."

Tori looked at him now. His tender gaze met hers. She couldn't read it. He wouldn't let her get that close.

"I'll see you later, Tori. Colt."

Tori just sat there and watched Logan walk off, but she had to stop him before she lost her nerve. "Dad, will you wait for me a minute?"

"Sure."

She called to Logan and he stopped on the sidewalk. He still stole her breath, in that rugged way he had about him. His sober expression didn't give anything away as usual. He was the expert on hiding his feelings. The only time he'd been completely honest had been when he made love to her. She knew he could care about her, if he let himself.

"I need to talk to you."

"We can talk later. Go be with Colt because he's leaving soon."

She nodded. "That's what I needed to tell you." She locked her gaze on those deep-set green eyes and rushed on to say. "Could you watch the ranch for awhile?"

He hesitated. "Are you going somewhere?"

She nodded slowly. "I'm going to Montana with Colt," she said, praying for him to ask her not to leave. But those words never came. She couldn't make him care about her. So she had no choice but to turn and walk away.

***

Two days later, barely forty-eight hours since Tori packed up and left Wyoming, and he still couldn't stop thinking about her.

Logan filled his time with work, cleaning out stalls just as he promised. Why hadn't he moved his horses back to his place? Then he wouldn't have to hang around here, filling his head with all the memories of the times they'd spent together.

Instead, he told himself he didn't want to move Domino, that the horse still had a lot of trust issues. At the top of the list, he missed one special woman. One time he was helping her to safety and then suddenly she was gone. How could Tori just leave?

He thought of his grandfather. This was when he missed the old guy the most. "Seems I keep messin' up, Nate. I sure could use some advice on this one."

Okay, so he was lousy at saying the right thing, but how could Tori just walk away? She'd had a bad time with Buckley, he understood that, but he wanted to be the one she needed. When he held her in his arms that last night...

Hearing a commotion, he went to Domino in the next stall. He opened the gate and took hold of the gelding's halter. "Hey, fella. I know you're miserable." He was, too. "But she could be coming back. She loves this place." He ran his hand over the horse's muzzle. Was that love enough to bring her back here? "She's been though some rough times. Remember, not so long ago you were having trouble dealing with things."

The horse bobbed his head. Logan might be able to lie to a horse, but he knew the truth. Tori wouldn't be back. The day she left, she'd come and packed up nearly everything in the cabin she'd brought with her six weeks earlier.

"Damn. Only six weeks."

"Only six weeks, what?"

He turned and saw Seth walking toward him. No, he didn't want to hear any `I told you so' from his neighbor.

"Nothing, I'm just having a conversation with my friend." He picked up the brush and began stroking the horse. "What are you doing out this way?"

"I've been looking for my friend." Seth leaned against the stall. "I heard Tori left."

At the mention of her name, Logan felt a tug at his heart. "A few days ago."

"So I take it she wasn't receptive to your declaration."

Logan didn't say anything. His hand moved in automatic rhythm.

"You did tell her you wanted her to stay, didn't you?"

Logan stopped his task and looked at Seth. "I didn't exactly get the chance. She told me she needed be with her family and recover from everything that happened here."

"Did she tell you that?"

"In so many words. She just said she was going back to Montana for awhile." He released a breath. "Her choice is for the best, Seth."

His friend arched an eyebrow. "Are you trying to convince yourself of that?"

"Maybe. I don't do well with relationships."

"That's because you don't try." He removed his hat and wiped his arm across his forehead, then replaced it. "For a big, badass ex-cop, you sure are deathly afraid of one petite woman."

Whoa. Those would be fightin' words if they weren't so damn true. Okay, so Tori Slater could bring him to his knees with just a look with those big brown eyes. "She's better off with her family. Plus she's building a relationship with her dad."

"And of course, she can't possibly have time for anything else, not a man she can build a life with, especially after a jerk like Buckley. There must be a man who could show her what she's truly worth.

Logan wanted to be the man to do that. He'd tried...

"And she loves this place," Seth said, as he rubbed Domino's nose. "Or did you miss all those little signals, too?"

"You seem to know a helluva lot about what Tori wants."

"I was paying attention."

Logan knew Tori wanted to make a success of the ranch, even run a herd, but that was before she found out he intended to take her grazing land. "She could still ranch here. I withdrew my bid on the land."

"Interesting." Seth released a long breath. "Again, did you tell her that?"

Annoyance crept over Logan's skin. "I told you, I didn't get the chance. Not between the Buckley mess and her packing up to leave."

Seth shook his head. "Are Clara and I the only ones who saw what was happening between the two of you?"

Their relationship was under scrutiny? Logan wasn't that convinced. "Once she gets settled back in Montana, she'll realize she's better off there."

Seth sighed a heavy breath. "Maybe I can enlighten you since I have a little experience here. I'll admit I did a lot of stupid things in my marriage with Ivy. She told me once I always made most of the important decisions because I thought I knew what was best for us." He paused as a faint smile appeared, then said, "That I never even asked her what she wanted. It's simple, Logan, just come straight out and ask Tori what she wants. Ask her to share this land, build a future together. If that's what you want. If you're not too afraid to take a chance. Because we all are afraid the person we love won't love us back. But you'd be crazy not to try with Tori."

Wanting to be hopeful, Logan gave a nod.

Seth continued, "I'm betting she's gonna pick a life here with you. All you have to decide is are you willing to take that chance and make a commitment to her?"

***

Tori loved being home this past week with her sisters, and at the same time she hated being home with her sisters. They were both married and crazy happy. Tori had to face all that sappy love stuff daily—which made her ache with loneliness. She missed the days and nights in Rachel's historic cabin.

She felt out of place. Even Colt had a life. Although she hadn't seen her around, Tori knew her mother was back in the area. Every time Colt got dressed up and said he was going into Bozeman, she knew he was seeing Lucia.

Everyone had a life, except her. She almost did, but then she'd walked away. Did she have a choice? Yes, but that meant she would have to stay and deal with Logan everyday. A man who didn't want her. So she'd moved back to Royerton, Montana, and the time was now to start a new chapter in her life.

Options existed. She could share office space at Temple Manor, with her sister Josie's event-planning business. She could run Tori's Designs from the large Victorian house that had been remodeled to hold weddings or small events. There were empty rooms upstairs for office space. That would give Tori a place to work, away from an apartment or the ranch with everyone watching her.

Tori walked up the steps to the wraparound porch where a chain swing and baskets of colorful flowers hung from the bead-board ceiling. The large oak door held an oval lead-glass insert and the name Temple Manor etched into the pane.

A smile crept over her mouth. This place was so Josie. She turned the brass knob, swung open the door and stepped across the threshold into a huge entry. She glanced around and caught sight of the hand-carved oak staircase leading to the second floor.

"Oh, my. It's all turned out so beautifully." She recalled the bad shape the place had been when Josie and Garrett bought it six months earlier.

The stained-glass window over the landing caught the sunlight coming through. She looked up at the high ceiling and found a magnificent crystal chandelier. Her artist's eye took over and she could begin to see the potential of this place.

All the rooms downstairs were the common rooms to rent for different social functions. She headed upstairs to the second floor. The wide hallway allowed for easy access to four bedrooms and a large bath. Two still carried remnants of peeling floral wallpaper from several different decades. It was the front bedroom she'd seen before that had interested her for her workspace.

She started toward the front of the house when she heard Josie's voice, along with someone else's. Tori waited out in the hall, not wanting to disturb them if a potential client was here.

Finally her twin sister came out of the bedroom along with another woman. An older woman with straight black hair styled in a blunt-cut that stopped just under her chin. Her olive-toned skin was flawless. Then the woman's ebony gaze met hers.

Tori froze, and a chill ran over her skin.

The older woman gasped, her hand resting on her heart. "Vittoria?"

A panicked looking Josie stepped in. "Ah, Tori, I didn't know you were coming in today."

Tori couldn't take her gaze off the beautiful woman. As a three-year-old, Tori had been too young to even remember her. How was she supposed to act toward a mother she'd never known?

"I wanted to look at the office space. You're busy now, so I can come back another time."

Josie held up her hand to stop her. "I know this is a shock, Tori, but you can't keep ignoring her. She's our mother. The fact she'd been practically held captive for the past twenty-five years wasn't her fault."

"I'm sorry." Her throat tightened and she swallowed hard. "I can't deal with this now."

Josie latched onto her hand and refused to let go. "You can't keep running away from this, sis."

"What is that supposed to mean?"

"I'm sorry, Tori, I know you've had a rough time lately with Dane. But we want to help you, and that includes Lucia."

In her head, she knew Josie was right, but her heart felt differently.

"What do you want me to do, have tea with her?"

Josie's blue eyes lit up. "I was thinking more along the line of a margarita."

Her twin wasn't much like her, not only in looks and coloring, but their personalities were just as far apart.

Maybe it was time to learn the truth. "Sure. What is it they say, it's five o'clock somewhere."

Lucia walked close, tears in her eyes. "*Mi hija,* I've missed you terribly. She waved her hand. "Sorry, I must speak English. Hello, Tori."

The backs of her eyes burned and she didn't know what to say. "Hello, Lucia."

Josie smiled. "That's a good beginning."

***

Later that day, Logan pulled his truck into the circular drive at the Lazy S Ranch. The sky was nearly dark, and he wasn't sure if he should have waited until tomorrow to see Tori. He hadn't called her, either. That would have given her an opportunity to tell him not to come, and tell him she didn't want to hear anything he had to say.

At least this way, she'd have to say those things to his face.

He turned off the ignition, climbed out and glanced around at the large compound. The outbuildings were painted a glossy white, along with the large barn. A half dozen ranch hands were busy with evening chores. Several horses were in the pasture enjoying the cool evening.

No wonder Colt chose here over the Colton Creek. This was a much bigger operation. Having second thoughts, he was about ready to leave when a man came out of the big three-story house.

About his same age, the tall man had sandy-colored hair and dark eyes. With a smile, he put a black Stetson on his head and hurried down the half dozen porch steps.

"Seeing the Wyoming plates on your truck, I'm guessing you're Logan McNeely."

"That would be me."

"Hi, I'm Vance Rivers, the foreman here. I'm also married to Ana, the oldest of the sisters. Welcome to the Lazy S." He offered his hand, and Logan shook it. "Colt has been raving about how well you've taken charge of Colton Creek."

He wished Tori was the one who'd talked about him. Guess he had to give her reason to. "Just doing my job. Is Colt around?"

"He's in the house, probably his office. Just let yourself in. It's the first left past the stairs off the entry down the hall."

Logan hesitated and glanced again at the house.

"If you're looking for Tori, she's not here."

Before Logan could worry she might have gone back to LA, Vance said, "She went into town to see her sisters, Josie and Ana." He sobered and looked down the driveway. "I thought she'd be back by now. I could call her."

"No, I can wait. I'd like to speak with Colt first." He said goodbye then walked up to the large porch. He reached for the knob on the oak door again wondering if he was making a mistake. Maybe Tori did belong here. Yet all he could think about was the time they'd spent together, talking, making plans for the ranch, holding her in his arms, making love to her.

Logan released a breath and stepped into a huge entry with high ceilings and hardwood floors. A beautifully carved banister led to a second floor. This was still better than anything he could offer her.

Colt came out of one of the doorways. He stopped when he saw Logan and grinned. "I was wondering when you would finally show up."

"I hope Tori feels the same way."

***

For the last three hours, Tori, her sisters and mother sat around a table at the Branding Iron Bar. The honky-tonk was authentic, with sawdust floors and unshelled peanuts on the tables and they served potent margaritas.

She glanced across the table to see Ana, who'd joined them after work at the high school.

Except for baby sister, Marissa, the group was one big happy family.

Both her older sisters had obviously accepted their mother was back. She'd listened to a lot of the story about her mother being held against her will by the threat of hurting her American family. And ever since her second husband, Vincente Santoya, died she had realized her dream of leaving Ciudad Juarez, Mexico, and returning to Montana... to her first husband and her daughters.

Tori's head was spinning with all the information, or was it the tequila? She glanced at the second pitcher on the table. She wasn't sure how to deal with any of this information.

Her thoughts turned to Logan. She had no doubt he would talk her through this with calm and ease. God, she missed him. So many times during the past week she'd hoped to hear from him. Hoped he'd cared enough to call her. He hadn't.

She took a sip of her tart drink and glanced across the table to see Lucia watching her, a soft smile on her face. Tori felt a sudden tightening in her chest. Why did this reunion have to be so hard? She had no idea how to treat her prodigal mother.

While the other sisters discussed the songs playing from the jukebox, Lucia leaned forward, and tried to speak over the music. "You are like me, *mi hija*. You don't have the Slater looks." Her mother smiled.

All these years Tori had felt out of place with her dark coloring and eyes, the opposite of her twin's lighter hair and the Slater blue eyes.

"You are so beautiful," she told Lucia. She was glad to see how much they looked alike, and nice to know that she might still have her looks even at fifty.

"*Gracias.* So are you. So are Analeigh and Josefina and Marissa." Tears welled in Lucia's eyes. "I'm just so happy to see you… again."

Tori felt emotions clog her throat, too. This was her mother. A mother she'd never had in her life. Josie was right; she had the choice to invite her in.

"So am I." And she meant it.

CHAPTER FIFTEEN

Nine o'clock came and went that night, and Tori hadn't returned from town. Logan's nerves about coming to Montana turned to uneasiness about Tori's whereabouts.

The only contact had been when Colt got a call from Lucia saying she and her daughters were all having a drink together at the local bar. That had been hours ago. That was when Colt decided to drive into town and see what was going on.

Logan pulled into the gravel parking lot of the Branding Iron Bar. He climbed out of his truck parked next to Colt's vehicle as Vance pulled in on the other side of him. Coming out of the bar was another large man who walked over and greeted Colt and Vance.

With a wave of his hand, Colt did the introductions. "Logan, this is Josie's husband, Garrett Temple. Garrett, Logan McNeely."

Logan nodded. "Nice to meet you.

"Same here." Garrett looked back at his father-in-law. "They're together inside, and that includes Lucia. And as far as I can tell there hasn't been any trouble."

Smiling, Colt said, "I've been hoping for this, that they would all talk with their mother."

"You can probably thank the pitcher of margaritas," Garrett told them.

"Likely more than one pitcher," Vance added and held up two fingers.

Garrett nodded. "But remember, we can't go barging in there like we did at Ana's bachelorette party."

Vance grinned. "I don't know, Ana was pretty happy to see *me* that night."

Logan's body stiffened. He didn't want to hear about their exploits with their wives. He wasn't so sure how Tori would feel about him showing up. "How's Tori?"

Garrett shrugged. "She seems to be enjoying herself," he said, and then turned to Colt. "I only caught a glimpse, but Tori and Lucia were talking."

Colt released a sigh. "Good. That's a start."

Vance stepped in. "Okay, so do we go in or wait out here? Either way, we'll be here when the party is over."

***

Tori smiled at hearing the stories from when she and Josie were babies.

"Josephina bossed you around even then," Lucia said with a swipe of her hand.

Josie raised her chin. "I was never bossy." Her twin's blue eyes sparkled. "I just knew what was best for Tori."

They all laughed, but then something drew Ana's attention, and she gasped as she pointed toward the door. Tori turned along with the others to see four tall men stroll into the room with that easy, loose-hipped gait that had every woman in the place staring, including her.

Vance, Garrett, and Colt and... Logan?

Lucia whispered in Spanish. "Oh, *mi corazon."* My heart.

"What she said," Josie agreed, mesmerized by the sight of the swaggering men.

Although all four men were worthy of a second and even a third glance, Tori had her sights only on Logan. He looked wonderful. His broad shoulders matched the others, but she thought he was the most handsome.

Even with his cowboy hat shading his face, she could feel the heat of his gaze. Her throat went dry, and her pulse raced. She'd missed him, missed the sound of his voice, his touch. How being in his arms felt, him holding her as if he'd never let her go.

But he *had* let her go.

Suddenly all the women at the table turned to her, but Josie was the one who spoke up. "Are you crazy? You left that hunk of a man back in Wyoming?"

Tori had no answer, but her heart raced in her chest. All she knew was that Logan had come to Montana.

Colt was the first to reach the table. He looked at Lucia and there was tenderness in his eyes, also a gleam. He winked then scanned the table. "Hello, ladies. Would you mind if we joined you?"

That set off giggles from the sisters as each man took his place next to his significant other.

Logan walked around the table a little slower, and when he reached her side bent close and whispered, "Hello, Tori," he said in a husky voice.

Tori ignored the warm tingle that rocketed down her spine. "Logan." Knowing her sisters were watching, she was trying to remain calm. "Funny seeing you here."

He shrugged, but his gaze never left hers. "I've heard so much about the Lazy S, I thought I'd come and see for myself. And I had some business with your dad."

Business. Suddenly, her heart sank into her stomach. "Oh, I didn't know you were still working for him."

"I'm not," was all he said as the jukebox began to play another song. He glanced at the couples around the table then pinned her with an intense look. "Dance with me."

The words weren't a question, so Tori took the hand he offered and went willingly. The floor was quickly becoming crowded, now including her sisters and their husbands. She let Logan direct her to a secluded corner then he drew her into his arms as Billy Currington crooned, *Let Me Down Easy.* The love song allowed Logan to hold her close.

He moved slow and easy with the beat, his hard body shifting against hers, causing her to shiver. She inhaled his scent, felt his heat even through his shirt and her blouse.

Oh, God, would her feelings for him ever go away? Only a week apart and she still craved his touch like an addict.

Okay, so she was thrilled he'd come to Montana, and had some hope he cared.

Not an expert dancer, Logan had trouble keeping time to the music as he listened to a song about a guy about to get his heart broken. This was the last place he wanted their meeting to take place. He wanted her somewhere alone. Somewhere he could give her a proper, personal greeting, and let her know how much he'd missed her. And having her this close was making it difficult to keep his hands from roaming.

His arm tightened on her back and pulled her against his body. She released a sigh as her fingers touched the back of his neck, teasing his hair.

She pulled back a little and tilted her head.

Those incredible midnight eyes locked on his. He was unable to draw his next breath, but he could remember every second they'd spent together.

"What business with Colt?" she asked.

"Not important now."

She shook her head. "It is important if it concerns Colton Creek." She sighed in frustration. "Look, Logan, I don't want to argue anymore, but I'll fight you." She pulled away and hurried off the dance floor.

He caught up to her back at the table, glad everyone else was still dancing. "Dammit, Tori, I didn't come to see Colt, not directly anyway." She made him feel as shaky as a teenage boy. "I came to see you," he blurted out.

He watched her swallow hard. "You did?"

He glanced around the crowded room. They couldn't talk here. Taking her hand he walked through the crowd and out the door.

"Wait, I should tell my sisters where I'm going."

Instead of relenting, he tightened his grip on her hand. He didn't want to chance losing her again. "Colt knows. I signaled him as we were leaving."

"What's going on? Why did all you guys show up here?"

"I was at the ranch waiting to see you. Lucia called Colt to tell him you were all having drinks. We only drove into town because Colt was worried you'd all been gone so long."

"You think I couldn't make it home?"

He shook his head, and his gaze shifted to the side. "I just wanted to see you. I was hoping you wanted to see me, too."

Tori closed her eyes and suddenly felt the effects of the margaritas. Why was she doing this? She wanted to be happy Logan showed up, but she didn't need more heartbreak. "That's the real reason you're here?"

His green eyes were difficult to read, like the man himself. "I was wondering how you were doing. Are you having any trouble from Buckley's father?"

She was about to speak when Colt and Lucia walked out of the Branding Iron. They had their heads together, looking as if they were sharing something very private.

Her father looked up and smiled.

"Glad we caught you before you left. It was too loud inside so I didn't get the chance to do the introductions. Lucia, this is Logan McNeely. He's been the caretaker of Colton Creek since his grandfather passed. Logan, this is my daughter's mother, Lucia."

Logan was taken aback by the woman's striking looks. "Ma'am." He took her hand. She looked like her daughters, Tori especially. "It's a pleasure to meet you."

"Lucia, *por favor*. I'm happy to meet you also. I want to thank you for helping Vittoria. For that I will be eternally grateful." She looked at Colt as she brushed back her straight hair, emotions evident on her face. "*Mi familia* is very important to me."

He nodded. "I'm just glad I was there to help, and that Buckley's going away for a long time."

Lucia nodded. "Will you be staying with us long, Logan?"

Stay with them? He caught Tori's glare directed at her father.

Logan knew he had a lot of explaining to do first. "That depends on some things I have to settle first."

Colt spoke up. He needed to give these two a push. "Well, we hope it's through tomorrow night because Lucia and I would like to extend an invitation to you for a barbecue at the ranch."

"Dad..." Tori looked embarrassed. "Maybe Logan has to get back to Wyoming. He has cattle and his horses to look after."

"Speaking of horses," Logan interrupted. "Domino misses you."

Colt watched his daughter's expression soften at the mention of the gelding. So there were some connections for her in Wyoming. Hopefully, one of them was this man.

"How is he doing?" Tori asked, her voice quiet.

"Like I said, he misses you."

"Who is Domino?" Lucia asked.

"An abused horse Logan rescued," Tori told her. "He's beautiful and so smart."

Logan shook his head. "I might have treated his physical wounds, but you saved him, Tori. I never thought he'd be able to be ridden again."

Lucia looked at her daughter. "I'm sure you miss him, too."

Tori nodded. "Yeah, I miss him. I miss seeing him every day, riding him."

Colt needed to give them another nudge, and he wanted some alone time with his former wife.

"I don't know about you two, but it's getting late." He looked at Logan. "You're welcome to stay at the house, son. We have plenty of rooms."

Tori looked ready to choke as she glared at him.

"I appreciate your offer, Colt, but if there's an extra bed in the bunkhouse, I'll stay there"

Colt arched an eyebrow. Wouldn't hurt the boy to suffer a little. "If you're sure?"

Logan nodded, then looked at Tori. "Possibly everyone would be more comfortable with that arrangement."

The older man nodded. "I take it you'll see that Tori gets home?" Colt looked at Tori. "Tomorrow, I'll send someone into town for your car."

Tori started to argue she could drive, but knew Colt's decision was for the best. "Okay." She glanced at her mother and saw the tears in her eyes. "I enjoyed tonight."

"So did I." Lucia took her hand and squeezed it. *"Gracias,* Vittoria."

"I'm taking Lucia home," her father said and lifted a hand in farewell. "I'll see you in the morning."

Tori nodded, wondering if this meant her parents were getting back together. "Good night, Lucia, Dad."

Tori watched them walk off hand in hand.

"She seems nice," Logan said.

Tori turned to Logan. "That's just it, I don't really know if she is or isn't. I don't want my father hurt."

"Their relationship is something they have to work out."

Logan took her hand and headed to the parking lot. He was nervous, had been since he arrived at the ranch. How would he begin to tell her how he felt? What if she wanted to stay here? Her family was all here, Montana.

He opened the passenger door and helped her inside. He went around to the other side, climbed in and closed the door, turning off the overhead light. For a few seconds he just sat there in the dark, with only the moonlight shining through the windshield.

"Logan?"

When he turned toward her, he reached out and cupped her face in his hands; then his mouth covered hers in a hungry kiss. She tasted like heaven, and it felt like years since he'd last kissed her. He nibbled and teased his way across her mouth.

She made one of those tiny whimpering sounds, making him only want her more. He needed more, too, and lifted her across the bench seat and onto his lap. She curled that sexy little body against him, and he felt his control slipping.

After a time, he tore his mouth away, but when he looked down into her eyes, he went back for another one of those long, sexy kisses.

"God, I've missed you," he breathed. "You'll never know how much."

She bit at his lower lip. "I thought I drove you crazy." With wiggling moves, she curled her cute little bottom over his lap and he began to work open the buttons on her blouse. All he wanted to do was push her down on the seat and take her right here in the truck.

"I've realized now, you're a good kind of crazy."

She smiled. "That's nice to know."

He lowered his head and kissed her neck, working his way down lower when someone tapped on the window.

"Oh, God," she groaned and buried her head against his chest.

Logan looked out to see a grinning Vance standing beside the truck.

"Hey, man, I was asked by my wife to give Tori her purse." He handed the small clutch bag through the window, but didn't leave. "Ana want to know if everything is okay."

"Everything is fine," Logan told him. "Tell her I'm taking Tori home."

"You want to follow us?" He gestured to an idling truck over his shoulder.

It wasn't a question as much as a request. "Thank you. Sounds like a good idea."

Vance nodded. "Tori, we'll see you back at the ranch."

"Okay, Vance," she said, her words blowing hot breath on his neck.

They watched Vance Rivers walk through the gravel parking lot and Tori murmured, "And you wonder why I came to Wyoming."

***

The next morning, Tori was awake about seven o'clock. She'd slept very little the night before after Logan brought her home. Thanks to Vance and Ana's escort, Logan had dropped her at the front door and continued on to the bunkhouse. They never got a chance to talk.

Well, she would find out his real reason for coming to the Lazy S, if it was the last thing she did.

After she showered and dressed, she went down the stairs and headed for the kitchen. In the large room, there were rows of white cabinets and dark countertops. A big table sat in front of the windows that looked out toward the pasture and the horses grazing. This had always been her favorite place in the house.

She heard familiar laughter and a plump middle-aged woman who was their housekeeper walked in. Kathleen Adams had been with the Slater family since Marissa was a baby. She was the woman who'd raised Tori and her sisters. And Tori loved her.

Her smile faded when she saw Logan was right behind Kathleen. He had on his standard jeans, boots and western-cut shirt. No one wore the cowboy uniform like Logan McNeely. And no one kissed like him either. Dang, she wanted him more than ever.

"Oh, you're up," Kathleen said, and then went to the stove and began preparing her breakfast.

"I only want some toast, please."

She looked back at the man who'd kept her awake most of the night. "Good morning, Logan."

He grinned and the skin at the edges of his eyes crinkled.

Her heart lodged in her chest.

"Mornin', Tori."

"Just because I'm not eating doesn't mean you can't. Kathleen makes a mean Spanish omelet."

"I know." He nodded. "I ate a big breakfast two hours ago with your father."

"Colt? He was here?"

"Where else would he be?" Kathleen asked.

"Well, I just thought..." She felt the heat on her face, thinking he'd spent the night with Lucia. "I don't know."

Logan went to the coffeemaker and filled two mugs. He took them to the table. "Sit down and have some coffee. I'll keep you company." He stood at the table and waited. Once she took a seat, he straddled the chair across from her.

Again, he smiled.

And again, her heart did a flip.

"What are your plans today?"

"I planned to help with the barbecue."

"I was hoping to spend some time together, so we could have that conversation we didn't get to finish last night."

Butterflies swirling in her belly. "Yes, we do need to talk."

Kathleen walked to the table and set down the toast. "You know, it's a shame you two are hanging around the house when today is so pretty. Why not go for a ride?"

Tori shook her head. "I'd planned to finish up some work."

Kathleen shrugged and glanced at the wall clock. "Ana has a short day at school, so she'll be walking in here a little after twelve. I give Josie until about ten o'clock to show up." The woman arched her eyebrow. "Are you ready to answer all their questions?"

After what she knew Vance had shared last night, Tori didn't want to face an inquisition from either sister. Tori looked at Logan. "Would you like to see some of the Lazy S?"

He stood and stepped closer, making her so aware of the man. He nodded.

"Good, then you tell me what business you had with Colt that brought you to Montana."

His gaze locked on hers. "There's only one reason I came here, Tori. To see you."

***

An hour later, Logan and Vance had saddled Ana's buckskin mare, Blondie, and one of Vance's horses, Rusty. By that time, Tori walked out of the house with a knapsack of snacks from Kathleen.

By the time she reached the corral, Vance was just finishing up giving directions around the ranch.

"You afraid I'll get him lost?"

Vance only smiled. "No, just adding some highlights about the property."

Tori had more to worry about than where they were going. She climbed on Blondie and Logan was right there to check her stirrups. She caught the gleam in her brother-in-law's eyes and suspicions gathered.

She'd known Vance Rivers most of her life ever since Colt took in the runaway boy at age thirteen. Vance had probably been in love with her sister, Ana, since the day he'd been found hiding out in their barn. They finally married last year.

"Why so interested are you planning to move here?" She looked at Logan. "Are you?"

He shook his head. "Just heard a lot about the Lazy S and wanted to see the operation." His green-eyed gaze met hers. "And see where you grew up."

She felt a grasp of hope, but quickly pushed it away. Don't be silly. She needed to think rationally. "Okay, then let's go."

He walked to Rusty. With the reins in hand, he grabbed the pommel and swung up onto the saddle with ease. Then he tugged his hat lower and nodded toward her. "Lead the way."

Vance opened the gate and she went through first and then Logan caught up with her on the trail. They rode across the lush green meadow, headed west toward the river. Finally, she kicked her heels into Blondie's sides and let her take off. Logan was right beside her and they raced along the bank until they came to the new-looking two-story log structure.

Tori slowed and they approached the wide porch where several Adirondack chairs were set out facing the majestic mountains.

"This is River's Edge. Ana and Josie came up with the idea of building a lodge for anglers, but it can also be rented out for corporate retreats and even weddings. Garrett's construction company built it. Ana and Vance were the first to be married here."

Logan shifted in the saddle. "The place turned out nice. Fits right in with the scenery." He glanced at the rushing river. "I bet the fishing here is great. Something like this could work in Wyoming."

Why was he talking about fishing?

Tori went on to say, "The important thing is the rent money pays for a lot of the ranch expenses and improvements. Also the income helps with Vance's horse breeding."

Logan didn't say anything for a long time, and then he turned to her. "I hear there's an old homestead around here."

Wondering what he was up to, she nodded slowly. "Yes, Sarah Millie Colton and George Slater settled here after they married."

"Could I see the place?"

She'd ridden out to the old cabin right after she came back home. In Rachel's diary, she'd written about how she worried and missed her eldest daughter, but understood she needed to start her own life. Wasn't that what Tori had done, tried to start over in Wyoming? At least, until she'd run back home again.

"Okay, let's go." She wheeled her horse around and headed along the river. After another twenty minutes they crossed a small wooden bridge. On the other side about fifty yards away she saw a small white structure.

"The place was practically falling down until Ana and Vance repaired it," Tori told him. "You have to get your water from a well, and the only bathroom is the outhouse."

"So this is the home George built? Is the barn still standing? The one that housed them and their animals that first winter."

Her gaze sharpened. "How did you know about that?"

Logan climbed down from Rusty. He didn't want Tori to think he'd invaded her privacy. "I read some of Rachel's diary. It was sitting out on the counter, and I found I was intrigued with her, too. She's your great-great grandmother. She's important to you."

Tori didn't say anything. She just climbed down and tied her horse to the porch railing then went to the door. She reached over the door frame, retrieved a key and unlocked the door.

Logan followed her into the dark space as she walked to the window. She pushed open the curtains and sunlight hit the small one-room cabin, with just enough space for a double bed, table and two chairs. Against another wall were the sink and some shelves for pots and pans and food. On the battered wooden floor was a new looking rug, and on the bed was a bright quilt.

"This is cozy, and looks like someone still lives here."

"Ana and Vance still come out here. And Josie and Garrett got stranded out here during a blizzard once."

Logan couldn't help but smile. "So this has become kind of a... getaway."

Tori didn't meet his gaze.

"I think our cabin beats this place by a mile."

She looked at him now, eyes wide. "Our cabin."

He nodded. "I spent enough time there... with you. I feel a connection to you there, especially after what we shared together."

She swallowed. "That's because you had this obsession to protect me."

He walked over and stopped in front of her, but he held back reaching for her. "Was having me in your bed that bad?"

Tori was frustrated trying to figure out what Logan wanted from her. "No, it wasn't. But you and I wanted different things." She raised her hand. "I realize I leaned on you too much. When I go back, I can't depend on you, or anyone else to be there for me."

When Logan opened his mouth to speak, she held up her hand and met his gaze head on.

"You need time to run your own operation." There she'd said it. "And now that you have the lease land, you can increase your herd."

He leaned against the counter and folded his arms across his chest. "Okay, I made some mistakes. The first one was, I should have told you about the lease right off, but it doesn't matter any longer because I withdrew my bid. It's up to Colt now. He can keep the lease, or let the State of Wyoming decide." He hesitated, then said, "Maybe we should get back to the house."

He started to leave and she knew she couldn't let him go. With a shaky hand, she touched his arm. "Logan, is that the reason you came to Montana? To tell me that you're giving up the lease?"

"It's part of it. That was just an excuse, the real reason was to ask you to come back to Wyoming. I want a partnership." He slowly turned toward her. "With you."

Tori's heart was pounding so hard in her chest she thought he could hear it. "So you want a business relationship?"

Those green eyes locked on hers. "I want more. I want you. I'm not saying it will be perfect, and I'm definitely not a perfect guy. All I know is, I don't want to live without you. Dammit, Tori. The ranch is not the same without you there." He began to pace the small space. "I know all your family is here, and maybe you should be, too." He stopped and looked at her, his lips in a tight line. "But I think we can build something good together."

She couldn't keep the tears from her voice. "Oh, Logan."

He reached out and touched her face. "Please, I don't want to make you sad. I know you've had it rough with everything going on. I want to help you through it all, with healing from Buckley and getting to know your mother again."

A tear dropped against her cheek, then her head dropped to his chest and she let them go.

"Ssh, baby. It's okay. I won't push you into anything. If you need more time, you got it. I'll wait for you."

Sniffing, she raised her head. "I need you. Only you, Logan."

His arms circled her. "From the first day, you've had me."

That made her smile. "I don't think so. I drove you crazy."

His fingertips caressed her cheek. "You were so beautiful; I couldn't stop think straight."

Her gaze lowered. "And I was a mess. I couldn't help anyone, let alone myself."

With a finger lifting her chin, he made her look at him. "We're all messed up a little, Tori. I thought you did very well with having a maniac after you. Look at me. I've lost everyone I've ever cared about." He drew a breath into his lungs. "I don't want to lose you, Tori. Ever. As hard as I've tried not to let it happen, I've fallen in love with you."

Again her ebony eyes filled with tears. "Oh, Logan. I love you, too."

He pulled her close and curved one hand around her cheek as he lowered his head. His mouth found hers.

His tongue glided over the seam of her mouth and she parted on a groan, drawing him closer, pressing her body to his as he deepened the kiss.

He drew back a little, his gaze aroused, but filled with such tenderness. She swallowed, wanting nothing more than to sink back into him. "Where do we go from here?"

"Anywhere you want to go, but you're not getting rid of me." He pulled her close again. "We're in this together."

CHAPTER SIXTEEN

Two hours later, Logan rolled over in the double bed in the one-room cabin and began to nibble on Tori's tempting neck. Again.

She shivered. "Don't start anything you can't finish, McNeely."

Logan smiled as he pulled her naked body against his, her cute little bottom snuggled up just right, giving him all kinds of sexy ideas. "You doubt me?"

She giggled as he ran his whiskered chin along her soft skin. They were both sated from lovemaking, but hey, he was more than willing...

Tori gasped and her body stilled. "No, we can't. "Everyone is waiting back at the house. Remember, there's a family barbecue."

She rolled over and faced him with those incredible midnight eyes, and he couldn't come up with a single coherent thought. He wanted to keep her here all to himself.

He reached out and stroked her silky black hair. "Just promise we don't stay all evening." He placed a kiss on her inviting mouth.

She arched an eyebrow. "And just how do we pull that off? Say good night and head upstairs to my bedroom?"

He couldn't help but grin. "Sounds good to me."

She sighed. "You know there'll be a lot of questions about us."

He loved this woman and he'd do about anything for her. "I have no problem telling everyone how I feel about you. I just wanted some time for us. Alone."

"We can't spend all our time in bed." She sat up holding onto the sheet for modesty. "Even you would get tired of that."

He sat up, too, and started to reach for her but pulled back his hand when he saw her tense. "Tori?" He then gently touched her this time. "Talk to me."

She turned, but her gaze was lowered. "What does 'together' mean? Is there a real future for us?"

He tipped up her chin and made her look at him. "I guess I'm not explaining myself very well if you have to ask my intentions."

"Yes. No." She sighed and her body slumped. "I'm not good at casual, Logan. And I know you want—"

He placed a finger to her lips. "I want you, Tori. I love you. Besides my mother when I was kid, I've never said those words to another woman." He released a slow breath. "I only wanted to give you time to see if you could put up with me. This ex-cop has a lot of rough edges. I'd also planned for a more romantic setting, and a ring to give you." He was so out of his element. Damn, Seth should have suggested he get a ring.

His gaze met hers and she was smiling. "All I can do right now is speak from my heart." His own pulse kicked up a notch. "I know... I'm sure you're the woman I want to spend my life with. I want to marry you, Tori."

With a gentle caress, she touched his face. "Oh, Logan, are you sure?"

"I'm sure I love you, Tori, and want to share my life with you. I'm not so sure you get a good deal with me."

"You're the best deal, and I love you so much. Yes, I'll marry you."

Relieved and grateful at the same time, he pulled her into his arms and kissed her; then kissed her again, each time a little longer and a little deeper until they were both lost in each other.

Tori in his arms--that was all he needed for a lifetime.

***

Colt stood at the edge of the patio watching for Logan and Tori. He'd gotten a call earlier from his daughter saying they would be there shortly. He smiled to himself, hoping the delay was good news. That Logan had the chance to plead his case to win her over.

Laughter rang out across the patio in the early evening. He looked around to see his eldest daughter, Ana, and his second born, Josie, talking with their husbands. The long table was set with numerous place settings, and a plate of chicken and ribs was prepared and ready to go on the grill. The set up looked like a typical family get together. And tonight, nearly the entire Slater clan would be here.

"You look happy, Colt."

He turned to see Lucia. Even after all these years, her beauty still took his breath away. Her mesmerizing black eyes and flawless skin with the creamy bronze hue got him every time. Her silky raven hair was cut straight just under her chin. She still reminded him of that shy girl he'd met back at the rodeo in Cheyenne.

He smiled. "You're back in my life. My doctor gave me a glowing report on my health, and I have a second chance, not only with you, but with my daughters. Oh, yeah, I'm a happy man."

Lucia came closer, slipped her arms around his middle and sank against his body. The gesture felt so familiar, yet different. New.

"I never stopped loving you, *mi marido."*

He blinked at her words. His chest tightened recalling all the lonely years. "I haven't been your husband for a very long time."

Her expression grew sad as she touched her heart. "You were always in *mi corazon*. All those years apart, I never stopped praying and dreaming about coming back to you."

Colt hugged her, thanking God she was here. "And now we are together once again."

He hated thinking about all the years Lucia had spent with another man. Yet after reading the private investigator's report on Vincente Santoya, he was grateful she'd survived those years. Santoya had been a cruel man, and feared by those who knew him.

Lucia had worked hard to protect their sons from Santoya's evil. He thought about Quintin and Rafael. They were grown men now, but he still wanted them to be a part of his life here in America. He wanted them to be Slaters.

Nothing remained of the Santoya drug dynasty in Mexico. Colt was happy about that, along with the fact Lucia never touched any of Santoya's drug money. She managed to make a living breeding horses and turned out to be a pretty savvy horsewoman.

In the past month, he and Lucia had discussed their future and the possibility of her bringing her thoroughbred horses here, and continuing her business. She wanted to put Mexico in her past. Although their sons had learned about their heritage, they were still adjusting to the news. And about who their true biological father was.

Colt felt a twinge of jealousy for all time he'd lost with his sons. But like his daughters, he'd been given another chance. He'd planned to do everything possible to bring this family together.

To some day have all of his children at the Lazy S Ranch, including Quintin and Rafael. Some legal maneuvering might be needed, but his friend and lawyer, Wade Dickson, was already putting the wheels in motion.

"Are you all right?"

She nodded. "I only wish my Marissa were here," Lucia whispered with such sadness in her voice.

Colt's thoughts turned to their youngest daughter. She'd only been a baby when Lucia was stolen away. "We will bring our *bambina* home soon. I promise you."

Lucia looked up at him; her eyes filled with tears. *"Gracias,* Colton. I'm so blessed I have another chance with you, and *mi hijas*."

"We're both getting another chance." He hugged her closer. "This time I'm never letting you go."

Josie walked over to her parents and pointed. "Well, look who finally decided to show up."

Everyone turned to see a couple holding hands as they walked up the slope toward the house. They suddenly stopped, moved into each other's arms and kissed.

Colt smiled. Logan McNeely was a good man for Tori. He was sure Nate would be happy with the match, too. "Seems they've made up."

Vance and Ana came to stand beside the others. "Must have been the detour by the homestead that did the trick."

"It worked for us," Garrett announced and Josie smacked him playfully. "Well, you can talk a lot when you're confined in a small space."

"Among other things," Vance murmured and that got him a jab in the ribs from Ana.

"We want Tori to be happy," Josie said. "And by the looks of them, I'd say they both are."

Tori finally looked toward the patio and said something to Logan. Suddenly, they both smiled.

Hand and hand, they reached the patio.

Josie hugged her sister first. "We knew something was going on between the two of you, so don't deny it."

Tori looked at Logan.

He announced, "Tori has agreed to marry me."

As everyone cheered, Colt hugged his daughter tight. "I've only gotten to know you again, now I'm losing you," he whispered only to her.

Tori pulled back and tears glistened in her dark eyes. "I will always cherish the time at Colton Creek."

He nodded, emotions clogging his throat. "I'm happy for you both." He looked at his future son-in-law. "I know Nate would be happy, too."

Tori shot a puzzled look at her father. "Did you know what Logan had planned?"

Colt shrugged. "When a man drives nearly three hundred miles, I knew he wasn't planning to go back to Wyoming alone. I just wish you'd be closer to home. So plan on a lot of visitors."

With a big smile, Tori nodded. "Will you be bringing Lucia?"

Colt smiled. The day was getting better and better. "The time has come to make this official."

Once he got everyone's attention, he drew Lucia to his side. Everyone looked at him, he began, "It took me a lot of years to realize what's important." He glanced at his soon-to-be wife again. He had no doubts how he felt about her, how he'd always felt about this woman. He was just happy his daughters were finding the same happiness.

"My family. I only wish Marissa was here tonight and everything would be about perfect."

Josie had told him earlier their baby sister's last message had said she was on a photo shoot.

Kathleen came out the back door, carrying a bottle of champagne. Vance went over to help her and popped the cork then began to fill the flutes lined in a row.

Colt took a glass and Lucia's hand. "First of all, your mother and I, want to toast Tori and Logan on starting this new chapter in their lives. Although I hate giving away another daughter, I'm happy for both of you."

He raised his glass. "To Tori and Logan and their future."

Everyone followed suit in the toast. After a few minutes of excited chatter, Colt called for everyone's attention again. "We have another reason for being here tonight." Again, he glanced down at the woman beside him. "I'm a very lucky man in more ways than I can count. In this past year, I've recovered from a stroke, and my estranged wife showed up on my doorstep. I call Lucia my wife because I know she didn't leave her husband and children willingly. Now she's back, and we decided we've spent too much time apart." He leaned down and placed a tender kiss on her mouth. "We're going to remarry."

Everyone was quiet a moment, then Josie said, "Like we didn't already know this."

That brought much needed laughter. Then Lucia spoke, the emotion obvious in her voice. "I don't expect to step right back into your lives as a mother figure, but I would like us to be friends if possible."

Tori nodded, and answered first. "I would like that, too. Will you help with my wedding?"

Tears filled Lucia's eyes. "*Gracias,* Vittoria. I would love nothing more."

Colt had more news. "There is something else we would like to talk to all of you about," he said. "Our sons, and your brothers, Quintin and Rafael. I want them here at the Lazy S where they belong. Where all Slaters belong."

There wasn't much of a response, then Ana spoke up, "If that's what you want."

Josie added, "Didn't you always want boys, Dad?"

Lucia looked up at him and said, "No one said this would be easy."

He smiled. "But we need to do it right this time." And he wasn't giving up until he had all his family together. He'd been given a second chance on life and love, and he planned to relish each day. He glanced at his wife and daughters.

Oh, yeah, he was one lucky man.

ABOUT THE AUTHOR

Patricia Thayer was born and raised in Muncie, Indiana, the second in a family of eight children. She attended Ball State University, before heading west. Over the years, she's made frequent visits back to the Midwest, trying to keep up with my family's numerous weddings and births!

She has called Orange County, California, home for many years. She not only enjoy the warm climate, but also the company and support of other published authors in the local writers' organization. For over twenty years, I have had the unwavering support and encouragement of my critique group. It's a sisterhood like no other.

Patricia has written for over twenty-five years and so far, she has authored over forty books. She's also had the honor of being nominated for both the National Reader's Choice Award and the prestigious RITA award and seeing her book 'Nothing Short of a Miracle' win a Romantic Times Reviewer's Choice award.

A firm believer in 'giving back', she's been a guest reader at elementary schools and lectured aspiring authors in high school as well as being a volunteer for the Grandparent Autism Network. A long-time member of Romance Writers of America, she has served as president and held many other board positions for my local chapter in Orange County.

When not working on a story, she might be found traveling the United States and Europe, taking in the scenery and doing story research while thoroughly enjoying myself with Steve, my husband. Together, we have three grown sons and four grandsons and one granddaughter. She calls them her own true life heroes. On rare days off from writing, you might catch her at Disneyland spoiling those grandkids rotten! When she wants some quiet time with her guy, they escape to their little cabin in the mountains and park ourselves on deck and let the world race by.

Other Books by Patricia Thayer:

--Slater Sisters' Series--

The Cowboy She Couldn't Forget 7/2013
Proposal At The Lazy S Ranch 11/2013
The Colton Creek Cowboy 12/2013
MARISSA'S STORY (COMING IN LATE 2014)
LOVE STRUCK COWBOY LUCIA AND COLT'S STORY (COMING SPRING 2014)

--Rocky Mountain Brides series--

Raising the Ranchers Family
The Sheriff's Pregnant Wife
A Mother for the Tycoon's Child
Single Dads Holiday Wedding
Her Rocky Mountain Protector

Printed in Great Britain
by Amazon

28572093R00169